ZOE EVANS

CHEER!

CONFESSIONS OF A ^Wannabe CHEERLEADER

Grrr!

Holiday Spirit

ILLUSTRATED BY BRIGETTE BARRAGER

Simon Spotlight
New York London Toronto Sydney New Delhi

This book is a work of fiction. Any references to historical events, real people, or real locales are used fictitiously. Other names, characters, places, and incidents are the product of the author's imagination, and any resemblance to actual events or locales or persons, living or dead, is entirely coincidental.

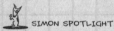
SIMON SPOTLIGHT

An imprint of Simon & Schuster Children's Publishing Division ★ 1230 Avenue of the Americas, New York, New York 10020 ★ Copyright © 2011 by Simon & Schuster, Inc. All rights reserved, including the right of reproduction in whole or in part in any form. SIMON SPOTLIGHT and colophon are registered trademarks of Simon & Schuster, Inc.

Text by Alexis Barad-Cutler

Designed by Giuseppe Castellano

For information about special discounts for bulk purchases, please contact Simon & Schuster Special Sales at 1-866-506-1949 or business@simonandschuster.com.

Manufactured in the United States of America 0311 OFF

First Edition 10 9 8 7 6 5 4 3 2 1

ISBN 978-1-4424-3362-5

ISBN 978-1-4424-3363-2 (eBook)

Library of Congress Catalog Card Number 2011934861

Thursday, December 29
Mornin', chowing on breakfast

Holiday Spirit Level!
It's Beginning to Look a Lot Like Drama

Ugh. I can't believe what just happened! So it's winter break—you know, a time when I'm supposed to be maxin' and relaxin' and just overall vegging out. And that's **EXACTLY** what I planned on doing—well, except for Grizzly practice, but that's fun for me—before The Phone Call. But instead? I'm having a major freak-out session. I mean, I should have guessed. Me? Being drama free? Ha-ha. Fat chance.

Something crazy just happened and I'm so confused about what to do. I was v-chatting a little while ago with Lanie, trying to make plans for later, when Mom knocked on my door.

"It's your dad," she said. "He needs to talk to you about something."

I'd heard the phone ring a few minutes before, but since Mom didn't scream for me to get it immediately

GIVE ME A
!!

(like she usually does when he calls), I figured it was for her.

"Ooh, must be serious," I thought. Because usually when Dad calls it's just to say hi, or to make me feel guilty about not being the genius daughter he always wanted. And then I was like, **PLEASE** don't let Dad and his awful girlfriend Beth be engaged.

I didn't want to pick up the phone. I tiptoed toward it extra cautiously, as if Mom was holding out a writhing snake. I could just see it: Beth would make me go shopping with her at the Bridal Barn and pick out an extremely gnarly bridesmaid dress with like, giant poofs for sleeves. Gross. Finally, I picked up the phone.

"Hey, Mads. You want to go with Beth and me to the Big Apple for the rest of your winter break?" asked Dad.

Phew. Wedding crisis averted. Wait. What? Did he just say, "Big Apple"? As in New York City? This is way better than Dad getting engaged. My brain said, "Heck

GIVE ME A 2!

yeah! When's the next plane?" Now this is
something I can get down with:
me, all bundled up in my adorbs
new winter coat
(christmas prezzie),
ice skating under the
Rockefeller tree. Eating
one of those big New York
pretzels . . .

But then I realized all that
daydreaming was just a big chunk
of brain fog because right after
my first thought of, yes please!
this annoying thing called Reality
hit: Hello! Madison Hays, aren't you supposed to be a
serious cheerleader? A C-A-P-T-A-I-N? On what planet
are you allowed to miss a whole week of practice—
especially during winter break? **NO
ONE** misses practice over break. It's
the best time to totally throw
yourself into
training. No tests to
worry about, no homework to
do. It's all cheer all the time. Or, in
other words: cheer Heaven.

GIVE ME A
3!

And when I say no one misses it, I mean not even the Grizzlies. We may not have any major games, but we do have an almost unhealthy amount of commitment to our team. My daydream of a snowy, carriage-ride-filled NYC trip began to dissolve into a puddle.

"So? Maddy? Whaddya say?" asked Dad, interrupting my thoughts.

I flopped down on my bed and sighed. "Oh, sorry, Dad. I was just thinking."

"Oh, so that's what it sounds like when the wheels spin in your head," Dad joked. Har dee har har.

"Um, shouldn't I ask Mom first?" Since she's my coach and all (oh yeah, and also MY MOM) I was pretty sure she'd have an opinion or two about me saying adios to the team to have a week o' fun with Dad.

"I already spoke to her—she wanted me to be the one to tell you, and she thinks you should go. You deserve a break, Madison."

THAT explains what they were talking about before I got on the phone.

Something is definitely fishy, though. First of all, Dad is always telling me I should be taking all advanced classes at school, plus weekend classes so I can "get ahead of the game." I'm pretty sure his idea of a great

GIVE ME A
4!

winter vacation for me includes math camp or learning Japanese—not frolicking down Broadway. Like, I've never heard him use the words "break" and "Madison" in the same sentence. (Unless he's wishing me good luck on a test, of course. Then he might say, "Break a leg, sweetie!" But that's totally diff.)

And also, what's up with the super-duper last-minute plan? Did he just wake up this morning and say, "Not only would we like to go on a spontaneous trip, but I want to take my daughter, even though we haven't been on vacation together since the time I enrolled her in the Little Tots program in ski school."

On the other hand, what if this is just a convenient way for Dad to ruin my cheerleading career? He's never been the biggest fan of the idea—especially since he had to listen to Mom talk about cheer the whole time they were married. And look how **THAT** turned out.

"Dad, I've got to think about it. We have a lot planned for this week's Grizzly practice." And we do: The Grizzlies are training for the Washington Get Up and Cheer Competition in the spring, and we're supposed to really rev things up this week. I know that the competition isn't the same as going to, say, a regional qualifier. But it's still a big deal for a novice team like us.

GIVE ME A 5!

Dad got all serious and said, "Well, it would be a nice opportunity for the two of us to spend time together."

Guilt trip much? I mean, it's true. Dad and I haven't hung out a lot recently (see ref to Tiny Tots Ski School trip). My eyes landed on the framed photo on my dresser of me and Dad on his old bike, with me in one of those baby seats attached to the back.

Guess Dad and I did have some good times way back when.

But then I realized, even if Dad was having a "my little girl" moment, this probably wasn't going to be just a trip for Dad and me alone.

"Dad," I said, "isn't Beth coming too? Having your girlfriend there isn't exactly just 'father-daughter bonding' time."

"Beth would really like to be your friend, Mads."

Super barf. Yeah, I can just picture Beth and me putting on face masks from the Body Shop and gabbing about boys and crushes. Maybe we'll download an awesome iTunes mix and start a hotel dance party! Ha! That's not happening. Not with "Business Beth." Does she even know HOW to vacation?

No room for a cheer skirt here!

GIVE ME A 6!

The trip is planned for Sunday. But luckily, Dad said I could tell him on Friday. Going to do some major soul-searching.

AFTER DINNER, IN MY MTV CRIB

It was a good thing I had plans to go to Lanie's this afternoon. I knew she would help me figure out my Big Dilemma. What I didn't realize until I arrived there, though, was that Lanie had some problems of her own: midget-size pop star problems.

I know, I know. Sounds crazy, but it's true. Lanie's mom answered the door with a grim expression on her face. "She's upstairs," she said to me, shaking her head. "But be prepared. It's bad."

I was like, "Weird. Lanie didn't mention anything being wrong when we were on the phone earlier." From the look on her mom's face, I was half expecting Lanie to be lying on her bed, staring up at the ceiling, like, Exorcist-style, going through one of her what's-the-meaning-of-life existential crises. Now that I think about it, THAT would have been a cheerier scene than what I actually did encounter once I opened her bedroom door.

Her room looked like Dustin Barker had walked in and exploded all over her walls, bed, and dresser. (sidebar:

GIVE ME A 7!

Dustin Barker is this celebrity whose photo is on the cover of every teen magazine. And in those photos he's always making über-fake kissy faces that have captions above them that read, "Do You Want to Know How to Be His Number One Girl?" or "How to Win Dustin's Everlasting Love." Every time he's shown on TV he's flashing a peace sign. Lame-o.)

At first I thought I was in the wrong room. Because MY Lanie is definitely not that kind of girl. Yeah, I know she's always had a secret crush on him, but I never expected to see a Dustin Barker shrine in her room. First of all, Lanie's the last person on earth to like the same guy as everyone else. In the entire time we've been friends I've never seen her glance at a teen magazine or listen to the radio. She'd much rather be reading some book of poetry. Also: Lanie doesn't really even do crushes. And second of all, even when she does like a guy, it's always someone really serious who wears all black and with combat boots and thinks not washing his hair makes a statement about his love of the environment.

When Lanes first told me about her obsession with Dustin Barker, I was like, "He's kind of cute. But really, I don't see the big deal."

"Big deal?" Lanie had said, looking at me like I was

GIVE ME AN 8!

wondering what the big deal of say, winning the lottery or breathing air was. She picked up her laptop to show me her Dustin Barker screen saver. "Just look at those kissable lips! That hair!" she swooned. "And whoa, can he dance!"

Ok, fine, so he's got (what everyone considers) "dreamy" hair that always falls down onto his left eye, and a constant smile that says, "Girl, you're the one for me." I know every girl in my school is gaga for him. I guess he's just not my type.

So here's the full extent of the Dustin Barker Damage: She has three different posters of him around her bed, a Dustin Barker scented candle (the label said "experience his essence" on it, which just sounds icky), and his autobiography (Dustified: An Autobiography) standing up on her dresser face out like a work of art.

I plopped down on her bed before giving her a dose of Maddy Reality. That's when I noticed the Dustin Barker bedspread. This was serious!

"Lanes, I thought that I was nuts when I fell for Bevan. But I didn't fill my room with his dirty gym socks. This?" I said, pointing to the Barbie-size Dustin Barker doll next to her bed. "This is a tad out of control."

GIVE ME A 9!

Lanie walked over to the Dustin Barker candle, her long black skirt trailing behind her. "True love is needs no explanations," she said, echoing one of his number one songs. "But there <u>is</u> a reason for all this. I'm getting myself psyched for when I meet him."

"Say what now?" I asked. Since when do teen heartthrobs make door-to-door calls?

She picked up the autobiography and held it to her chest. "He's coming to the Book Worm to do a book signing. You didn't hear about it?"

I shook my head. "Nope. I don't get the Dustin Barker fan club e-mails."

"Well, anyway. I'm going to meet him!" she swooned. "I don't care how many hours I'll have to wait on line. I'm even going to give him a pen to sign with so I can have something he's touched." She had a crazed look in her eyes.

"I'm legitimately worried about your health."

GIVE ME A 10!

"It's perfectly healthy for a girl to have a celebrity crush. Dr. Drew even said it was 'aspirational.'"

"Ok, now I'm <u>really</u> worried. Lanie Marks does not watch VH1 or MTV. She watches PBS."

"I know, I know," sighed Lanie. "But I didn't have a choice. How else would I watch the Dustin Barker Little Bit o' Christmas special?"

I couldn't help but laugh. "But that's just it! <u>My</u> Lanie also doesn't like superfamous pop stars."

Lanie leaned against the giant Powerpuff Girls pillow that has been on her bed since we were four. "Well, maybe this is a part of Lanie you didn't know. Or maybe I'm the new Lanie."

"Whatever you say, Lanes. I'm here for you when he breaks your heart."

"Thank you," said Lanie. "So. Let's talk about you. What's new?"

I told Lanie what the sitch is, hoping she'd help me solve this mess.

"Whoa. That's amazing!" she said, before I even mentioned the dilemma part. "When do you leave?"

"Well, I haven't exactly decided if I'm even going yet," I said. "That's the thing. I don't know if it's a good idea for me to miss Grizzly practice. Or even if I want to be on a vacation with my dad and Beth, you know?"

GIVE ME AN
11!

Lanie rolled her eyes like she was trying to talk sense into a three-year-old and took a seat next to me on the bed. "I'm going to make this easy for you, Mads." Her expression was dead serious. "You're going."

"I am?"

"You don't have a choice! A free trip to New York? Um. Yes, please."

I grabbed Lanie's ratty old teddy bear and played with the loose button on its shirt. "I know! That's what I thought at first," I said. "But then I realized, what kind of example will I be setting for the team about commitment, you know? I've been droning on and on about how we need to make the most of every night's practices, and take as much time as possible to train over break. And now I'm just going to be like, 'Peace out, Grizzlies'?"

Lanie listened patiently. "It's New York, Mads. Fashion capital of the world. Remember 'fashion'? Your favorite thing after cheer and moi, of course. Do I really need to remind you?"

"You forgot Bevan," I said. "He's up there too." Sigh. Bevan. I haven't seen him for over a week and I'm having withdrawal.

"Fine, he can share my pedestal," said Lanie. "But no more making fun of my crush. Anyway, I hear you about

GIVE ME A 12!

being a slave for cheerleading and all, but this is a great chance for a fun vacay. And also, since your dad and Beth will want some alone time, they'll probably let you do your own thing a little."

I have to admit I hadn't thought about that before she mentioned it. Being on my own in the city of my dreams? That would be awesome. We'll have to see about that. . . . Dad's usually a strict guy, but then again, I haven't ever hung with him and a serious girlfriend 24/7.

I just hope that the rest of the team agrees with Lanes. I haven't even spoken to Jacqui about it yet. I'm too afraid of her being disappointed with the idea that I'm leaving her alone with the team for a week. Then again, maybe the fact that I'm feeling guilty about it means I've made my decision. . . .

When I got back home from Lanie's, Mom was up watching some black-and-white movie with Marlon Brando in it (he's one of her favorite actors of all time). Even though he is from the age of the dinosaurs, I guess he was kind of cute back in the day. Maybe teenage girls had posters of him all over their rooms too (if posters even existed back then).

Mom put the movie on pause. "Oh, honey, close the door quickly, please. It's freezing outside!"

GIVE ME A
13!

Mom is always cold no matter what season it is. But she's right—it's colder than usual today.

I opened the kitchen cupboard to grab some Swiss Miss.

"So, have you decided? Are you New York bound?" Mom asked, holding her blanket close to her body with one hand and her mug of tea in the other as she shuffled into the kitchen.

I put up some hot water. "Well, I have pretty much T minus five seconds to decide," I told her. "I want to go. Lanie thinks I should go. Dad thinks I should go, obviously. But I'm worried about the Grizzlies."

She leaned back against the counter next to me. "I know that you were really looking forward to practice this week. But think of all the fun you'll have. We'll all miss you here, but trust me, we'll be fine." She took a sip. "What did Jacqui say about it? Did you talk to her?"

"No, not yet," I said, licking some of the cocoa powder off my hand. "I'm going to catch her first thing before practice tomorrow and let her know what

GIVE ME A 14!

I'm thinking. If she acts the teeniest bit upset about it, though, I'm not going."

"Madington," Mom said, shaking her head. "You have to make the decision that's right for you. Don't worry about other people so much."

"I know, I know," I muttered.

But still, I'm not convinced. Everything hinges on how Jacqui and the Grizzlies react.

Later on I called Bevan to give him the update too.

"Awesome!" he said, when I told him about the trip. "I remember you saying that you haven't been on a vacation with your family in a while."

It's true, I did mention that. I just didn't think it would happen so soon. I guess I was picturing something over the summer— but even then, that would interfere with cheer. I can't really win, I guess.

"Yeah, coming from the guy who goes on three big family vacations a year. I knew you'd understand."

GIVE ME A 15!

This year Bevan has already been to Aruba and Florida, and they've also taken a family ski trip. And the year isn't even over yet, technically.

"I wouldn't consider visiting my grandparents' condo in Florida a vacation," said Bevan.

"Uh, spoiled much? Anywhere with palm trees and sun is a vacation to me."

"Yeah, yeah. Anyway, I'm happy for you. I mean, I'll miss you, but still. You'll have a blast in New York. I'll tell you some places to hit up."

Of course he's already been to New York. Probably, like, ten times.

"Cool. But I'm not 100% positive I'm going yet. I want to see what the team thinks first."

"I guess that makes sense," said Bevan. "The team comes first, right, Mads?" I know he was being sarcastic, but that's pretty much how I really feel.

The team **DOES** come first. So how can I even consider abandoning them?

GIVE ME A 16!

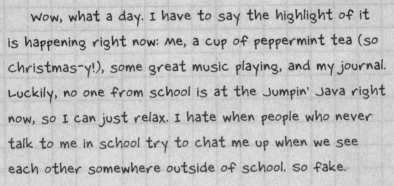

Wow, what a day. I have to say the highlight of it
is happening right now: me, a cup of peppermint tea (so
christmas-y!), some great music playing, and my journal.
Luckily, no one from school is at the Jumpin' Java right
now, so I can just relax. I hate when people who never
talk to me in school try to chat me up when we see
each other somewhere outside of school. So fake.

Last night I dreamt that my squad was drowning
in a big ocean, and they were all calling for me to save
them. Ian McClusky had sunk right to the bottom
of the ocean because of all his football muscle. And
Tabitha Sue was waving her pom-poms frantically
before she fell underwater too. Jared did a swan dive
before realizing he couldn't swim, and Katarina was
saying, "Help me!" in Russian. I woke up sweating and
realized after a few moments that it was a bad

GIVE ME A
17!

dream. Then I was like, whoa, Captain Obvious—someone's freaking out about leaving the team behind. Couldn't my brain have tried to be a little bit more mysterious and deep? I decided I definitely had to tell the team about my New York plan before my nightmares got worse.

I texted Jacqui right after I woke up to ask her to meet me a couple of minutes before practice in the gym. I've always kind of liked the emptiness of our school over break. It's like you can still hear the echoes of lockers slamming and kids shouting in the hall, long after everyone has left for winter vacations. But today, as I pushed open the heavy doors to the gym, the school felt **TOO** big and empty. I could hear my heart beating, thunka, thunka, thunka. I can't believe I was so nervous just to talk to my friends! But I really was worried that:

a) Everyone would think that I'm not a good captain.

b) Something bad would happen to the team because I wasn't there (hmm, big ego much?).

But one thing at a time. First I had to talk to Jacqui. I know she can totally handle the squad on her own, but me not being there will def mean more work for her. As I walked toward the bleachers on our side of the gym, I decided that if she said my going was ok, I would stay late with her after practice today

GIVE ME AN 18!

and come up with a plan for the week for her to do with the squad. And I would owe her big-time, of course.

Jacqui was sitting on the lowest bleacher, digging around in her ginormous bag. "I got you, my pretty!" she said, imitating the Wicked Witch of the West, and holding up a safety pin.

I sat down next to her. "Uh, should I be worried about that pin of yours? Do you want me to take it down? Because you know me, I can seriously kick some safety-pin butt if needed."

And it's true. I know my way around some sewing supplies.

"No." She frowned. "'S ok. Just lost a button on my shirt. Ugh, and I hate this shirt too, but it's the only thing that's clean."

"Here, let me help you with that." I took the pin and performed some of my fashion design magic. When I was done, her shirt was back together and you couldn't see the pin at all.

Jacqui took out a pocket mirror to check it out. "Nice, Mads, I owe you one! It looks good as new."

"You're welcome," I said. "And . . . speaking of favors, I kind of have a big one to ask you." I rubbed my sweaty palms against my sweatpants as I geared up

GIVE ME A 19!

for her reaction. I told her about Dad asking me to go away with him and how it was super last-minute. "And I completely understand if a whole week alone with the squad is too much to handle. I don't know if I could do it alone either," I said.

I think I was expecting her to be mad, or annoyed. I wouldn't be overjoyed if she sprang a last-minute trip on me, either. But instead, she just patted me on the back and said, "Cool."

"What?" I asked, amazed.

"Seriously?" said Jacqui, smiling. "It is so not a big deal. Don't worry, I got your back."

"Are you sure?" I asked. I couldn't believe it had been that simple. I thought for sure she would need some time to think about it at least.

"It'll be great!" said Jacqui. She rubbed her hands together like an evil villain. "With you gone I can be extra tough on them."

"Are you calling me a softie?" I asked jokingly.

Jacqui smiled coyly. "Only a little. Remember how drill sergeant-y I was when I first got to the team?"

I nodded, thinking back to last September, when Jacqui first joined our team. The squad didn't even know what hit them. I knew how to cheer and dance, but I hadn't been part of a squad before, so pushing

GIVE ME A 20!

others to their limit wasn't really my thing. Jacqui
came in and changed that. She taught us all what
a real warm-up was—leaving us sweating and in an
insane amount of pain when she was through with us.
We're in such better shape now. Sometimes I can't
believe how far we've come as a team in so little time.
Even the Testosterone Twins have learned some
coordination.

As if on cue, Ian and Matt came strutting into the
gym, wearing practically identical muscle T-shirts and
bandannas. Matt stared at one of the Titan girls, who
was practicing her round-off.

Jacqui rolled her eyes. "These guys especially need
a little kick in the butt," she said, motioning in Ian and
Matt's direction.

I was so relieved. I really am lucky to have Jacqui
as a co-captain. I mean, without her this trip wouldn't
even be remotely possible. It was only a couple months
ago that I was the only captain of the team. And if
that were still the case, who would take over if I went
away? (Besides Mom, I mean . . . but that would be
totally out of the question.)

Even though Jacqui said she was cool with it, I
was still worried about what the squad would say.
I told Jacqui I'd tell them at the end of practice.

GIVE ME A
2!!

I didn't want to ruin their upbeat mood—they've been doing great all week on this thing Jacqui and I came up with. Inspired by the awesome dance moves from the Titans' routine from the qualifier, we decided to create a routine for the Grizzlies to learn over break that paired the new cheer moves they've learned with lots of dance. Ian and Matt were less than thrilled with having to learn more dance moves, but Jared (of course) was psyched.

Practice began with a few laps around the gym and then some stretching. I had the idea to incorporate a little yoga into our stretches—to really elongate the body. I've taken a bunch of classes with Mom, so it was easy to figure out some basic moves that the squad could handle.

"Tabitha Sue, straighten your leg," I instructed, as I walked around the mat.

GIVE ME A 22!

"This is as straight as my leg goes," she said. "And all the blood is rushing to my face. Is that normal?"

"Ummm . . . just breathe it out." That's what my yoga instructor always said, anyway.

Jared had already resorted to child's pose, which is the position where you kind of look like you're praying. It's a great position to rest in after a tough pose, but I could tell Jared was just trying to get away with some relaxation during stretching.

"Ahem," I said, my hands on my hips.

"What?" asked Jared innocently.

"Up, Jared," said Jacqui, still in downward dog position.

I heard someone snickering nearby and turned my head: It was Clementine Prescott. Somehow she had a deep golden tan, even in winter. "What's this? Yoga for dummies?" she said with a grin.

I tried to ignore her but had a feeling she wouldn't leave unless I acknowledged her presence. "For your information, we're trying something new. Mixing it up. Maybe you guys should try it."

I turned back to the Grizzlies. "Ok, everyone, do your sun salutations."

"Say hi to the sun for me," she sniffed.

"Go back to the mall," said Ian.

GIVE ME A 23!

As soon as Clementine walked away, Ian got up from the mat. "Hey, everyone," he said. "Guess who I am?" He started prancing across the floor with his hands on his hips. He gave his imaginary audience a serious stare, then shimmied down to the floor into a split (or his version of a split).

"That was a pretty good Clementine imitation," said Tabitha Sue.

"But Clementine would remember to point her toes in that split," said Jacqui.

"I was doing an imitation—not an actual cheer," growled Ian.

"I think Ian likes to dance more than he lets on," said Jared.

"Do not, Twinkle Toes!" barked Ian.

Jared made a face. "Call me names all you want. I'm proud of my dance ability. Speaking of," he said proudly, addressing the team. "I've been DVRing So You Think You Can Dance, and I can basically do all the moves on the show."

"You mean, like the part where the team bows at the end?" quipped Ian.

Jared continued, ignoring Ian. "I was thinking Jacqui and Maddy might want to add some of my moves to our new routine. Watch. And. Learn."

GIVE ME A 24!

Before we could look away, Jared did a series of head bobbles and awkward kicks, and even attempted to break-dance. It was pretty brutal to watch. I could see Jacqui was trying to hold back giggles.

"Thank you for um . . . that," I said to Jared. "We'll keep some of those moves in mind." Uh . . . yeah, for when we need a good laugh.

"Ok, ok, guys," said Jacqui, clapping her hands together. "Enough playing around. Let's get back to our own routine, shall we?"

Immediately, everyone got into formation. That's something I really love about our team. They know when they've had enough goofing-off time and when it's time to get serious.

Jacqui continued to drive her point home. "You guys say you want to be like the Titans?" she asked. "Well, you can't get there"—she pointed across the gym to where Clementine and Marie were demonstrating advanced basket tosses to the rest of the Titans—"without starting here."

I caught Tabitha Sue staring at them in awe, her eyes glazing over as one of the Titan flyers was propelled upward into a pike, and as she started to fall she went into a toe-touch before landing in a cradle. Then Tabitha Sue seemed to snap back to attention and

GIVE ME A 25!

turned to the rest of the team. "Let's go, guys," she said. "No pain, no gain."

Jacqui and I gave each other a look that said, "We've created a monster—and that is totally awesome."

Which got me thinking—I guess the team **WILL** be just fine without me.

We practiced the routine until our limbs felt like they might come off. Everyone was red in the face from the millions of jumps we'd been practicing. As I bent over my knees to catch my breath, I saw that some of the squad were already heading toward the locker rooms.

"Wait!" I shouted. "I need to ask you guys something." Four heads turned to me at once.

Jacqui just smiled, like what I was about to say was no big deal.

I took a deep breath. "My dad invited me to go to New York with him next week, but I wanted to make sure you'd be ok if—"

"I love ze New York!" squealed Katarina, not letting me complete my sentence. "Ze Big Apple! I always have dreaming of going there. You can go to museum!"

"Oh, Madison, there are so many Broadway shows you have to see! I'll tell you everything you need to know," said Jared.

GIVE ME A 26!

"I know." I beamed. "So are you guys saying you don't mind if I go?" I asked.

"Are you kidding?" said Tabitha Sue dreamily. "You have to go! Just think of the celebrity sightings."

"There's so much I want to do there," I admitted. "But what I'm really excited about is the fashion." As I thought about it, I started to get even more excited. "It's the home of <u>Vogue</u>! And Fashion Week!" I exclaimed.

"And the Rockettes," said Matt, wiggling his eyebrows suggestively. He closed his eyes and sighed, with a smile. "Ah, the Christmas Leg Spectacular."

"Seriously," said Jacqui. "You have problems. But speaking of legs, none of you are leaving without stretching first. I don't want any injuries while Maddy's gone."

Everyone groaned.

Everyone except me ☺. I was so relieved that my teammates were cool with my announcement that I could have stretched for hours.

Everyone who I've asked about my going is practically pushing me onto that plane. Hmm . . . either my family and friends really want to get rid of me for a week, or I look like I'm in **MAJOR** need of a vacation.

Whatever the reason, all signs are pointing to me

GIVE ME A 27!

going. So there. There is no reason **NOT** to say yes to this trip.

Jacqui and I stayed late as planned to go over what the team will do the week I am gone. The Grizzlies are in for a grisly surprise (Get it? Ha-ha.). We planned one day that will be intensely tumbling based, another with tons of jumps (not so diff from today's practice), and another that's going to be an insane amount of dancing. Not to mention the mandatory laps that Jacqui is planning on having them do.

"Don't worry, they'll be fine," she assured me, as I looked over the week's roster.

"Just promise me, if someone passes out, you'll take it down a notch. Ok?"

Jacqui laughed like the Wicked Witch of the West (she was really getting into character today!). "Just kidding. I know when to lighten up."

"Suuuure you do," I said.

So I finally called Dad to tell him my decision.

"Oh, Madison! That is just delightful news!"

Delightful? Who says that?

"Yeah," I said. "It will be fun."

"Well, thank goodness you said yes, because I have to admit—I've already bought the ticket."

"Daaad!" I whined. "That's a lot of money wasted if I had said no."

GIVE ME A 28!

"Good thing I had a feeling you'd say yes," he teased. "I'm going to call Beth right now!" I could hear him smiling on the other end of the phone.

Ah, yes. The only bummer part of the equation—a whole week with Beth. Well, as Jacqui says, no pain, no gain, right?

Ok, well, off to Evan's now to tell him the big news. Fingers crossed he takes it as well as everyone else (even though something inside tells me that's not going to happen). . . .

LATER, COMFY ON MY COUCH

The walk to Evan's from the coffeehouse was fuh-reezing. When exactly did Port Angeles turn into Antarctica?? I passed the familiar streets leading to his house, noticing as I got closer that the lawns were getting bigger and bigger and the houses were taking up more space on them. The two of us used to walk to his house after school almost every day—way before I joined the squad. Sometimes we'd race there, making up dorky rules like, "You can only hop the rest of the way," or "Quack like a duck as you're running." But that was a loooooong time ago. As I took the last turn on the way to his house, I realized I couldn't even remember the last time I'd been to Evan's! It dawned on me that we

GIVE ME A 2Q!

really haven't been seeing much of each other. Maybe
it's because of how much time I spend cheering, or
maybe it's because Bevan and I have been hanging out a
lot. Or maybe it's because we've grown apart since our
racing days.

I reached up to
knock on the door in
the one area that was
not covered by the
enormous Christmas
wreath his mom puts up
every year. I waited, but
no one answered. Boy,
was I grateful for my
new black knit gloves
with sparkles on them.

So Cool
they're HOT

They're so cool because you can wear them either
fingerless or the regular way.

Finally (what felt like ten years later) he answered.
His eyes seemed to soften a little when he looked at
me. Weird.

"Sorry," said Evan, closing the door behind me. "I
didn't hear the doorbell."

The speakers were blasting with the telltale sound
of his favorite game.

GIVE ME A
30!

"Oh, don't worry about little ol' me freezing my brains off out here," I said, shivering, and headed for one of the old-fashioned radiators to get the blood flowing back in my fingers.

"It's time for some hot chocolate, STAT. Remember, our tradition?" I asked.

Winter break has always been a big Evan and Maddy week. Every year we've made, like, six different types of hot chocolate and had a blind tasting. The highest rated hot chocolate recipe would accompany us as we watched cheesy Christmas movies.

Evan smiled. "I thought you forgot. We didn't exactly make plans," he said, with a bit of sarcasm in his voice.

"Gee, I didn't know we were so formal."

He shrugged.

We went into the kitchen to start pulling some spices. I'm a big fan of cinnamon in mine, and he is all about the vanilla.

GIVE ME A 3!!

"Well, to tell you the truth," said Evan, "I already ordered a bunch of DVDs for us to watch. I figured either you'd come over, or you wouldn't, but tradition's tradition. Gotta have my Christmas movie fix."

I winced. I hate to disappoint good ol' E, especially since I'm the one to bring up our hot chocolate and movie thing. And now I had to cancel it. I'm a monster.

"Actually," I said, "that's kinda why I stopped by. There's a going to be a bit of a change in plans this year. See, I'm actually going away with my dad for the rest of break. We leave on Sunday."

"Oh," said Evan, obviously surprised. He was quiet for a few beats. "That's cool," he said finally. I could hear the little squeak in his voice that always comes when he's disappointed.

"Yeah, we're going to New York City. Me, Dad, and Business Beth." I made a serious/mean face as I said Beth's name, hoping Evan would laugh at my Beth imitation like he normally does.

He didn't. Ugh.

I stirred some milk into my drink to fill the silence.

"So, just wondering, how long did it take you to tell me you were leaving? I'm surprised you didn't just call from the plane at this point." He was trying to sound like he was just joking, but I could hear that he was annoyed.

GIVE ME A 32!

"I'm not leaving. It's a vacation. And it was super last-minute. I just decided I was going about an hour ago," I said.

"Whatever," said Evan, playing with a button on his shirt (which, BTW, looked like he had raided a hippie's closet—it had those oversize cuffs and a huge collar. Saturday Night Fever much?).

"I thought you'd have to stick around since you're a captain," he said. "At least, Katie told me that this week is one of the most important practice weeks of the year."

He knew he was dealing me a low blow. Mentioning Katie Parker is his way of hitting a nerve, and trying to make me feel guilty about cheer in the process—well, that's a double hitter. Boy, he's good.

"Well, yeah, it's not something I want to make a habit of, but Jacqui and the squad are being cool about it. But seriously, thanks for _your_ support," I added sarcastically.

Despite the Negative Nancy mood Evan was in, I ended up staying to watch movies with him. But things between us were definitely awkward. He didn't share the blanket on his couch with me like he usually does. And he didn't laugh at any of the jokes I made about the movies. The whole rest of the night he just seemed to actually be . . . upset. Weird, right? I knew he'd be a **LITTLE** bummed that we won't be hanging out like we usually do every year. I am too. But now that I'm thinking about the way he acted today, I'm kind of thinking, what gives him the right to give **ME** a guilt trip? It's not like I'm the only one who's been busy—he's been doing stuff too: working on SuperBoy and hanging out with Katie. Although come to think of it, I haven't heard about them hanging lately. Maybe something happened? Which could explain his 'tude. Maybe he's a cranky-pants in general **BECAUSE** he and Katie actually haven't been hanging out as much. I know that they aren't, like, a couple or anything, but he definitely likes chilling with her. So maybe he was hoping I'd be a distraction this week . . . perhaps should try to get some info from Lanie on this? Nah . . . she hates being in the middle. Grrr.

I don't know. I guess what's really bothering me is that in the old days, I wouldn't have had to guess at

GIVE ME A
34!

what was bothering him like I am right now. AND, in the old days I used to be able to just call him out on things and say, "Ok, what's your deal?" But now it doesn't feel the same. All this guessing about his feelings is making me feel a little nauseous. Or maybe it was all that hot chocolate. Ugh.

GIVE ME A 35!

Holiday Spirit Level:

Rah, Rah, Romance!

I kinda can't believe it's New Year's. The whole idea of starting a new calendar year in the middle of the school year just feels so, well, lame. I mean, sure we get a break and all, but we come back to school in the same place, taking the same classes, with the same people. I don't know, it just feels like the new year should bring about change. BUT, no time to worry about that now. Mom and I will have plenty of time to deal with that later on tonight when we usher in the ball drop. (And my insides squirm with delight seeing the Big Apple on TV and knowing that in just one short day I'll be there!!)

Now there are more important things at hand. Like the fact that I just came back from my Bon Voyage date with Bevan. It was his idea that we get together one last time before I leave for New York. So sweet,

GIVE ME A 36!

right??! We went to see a cute romantic comedy with Reese Witherspoon, and when we got there he was like, "You find seats. I'll get snacks."

I got us two seats in the middle of the theater, but near the aisle. I don't know why, but that's my usual movie spot. I like the view, but I hate that we always have to stand up to let other people squeeze past so they can get to the middle of the row. When he came back from the concession stand, he handed me my favorite candy (gummy worms, of course).

"How did you know?" I asked.

He smiled slyly. "I pay attention to these things," he said.

As soon as the previews were over, I felt his hand creeping toward the edge of my seat. I was like, um . . . am I supposed to put my hand over his??? I was too nervous to do it, though. Finally, after the opening credits, he made The Big Move, and put his hand over mine. We stayed like that the entire movie. About halfway through the movie, I put my head on his shoulder and noticed he'd put some cologne on. Fancy, fancy!

GIVE ME A 37!

When we walked out of the theater, it was serious glacier weather outside—way too cold to walk home. So Bevan asked if his mom could come pick us up and drive me home. Luckily, she didn't want us to turn into icicles either, so she came in less than five minutes. But when she pulled up to the theater parking lot in her enormous pickup truck, everyone was staring. It's not every day that you see a woman who is as pretty as a J. Crew model driving a monster truck. She even wears these huge work shirts that cover most of her body.

Watch out, road!

She's so cool that when we got to my house she announced she would "take a little spin around the block," which obviously meant she wanted to give us our privacy while we said good-bye. Only mildly embarrassing.

As Bevan and I stood by my door, I think I was waiting for him to tell me that he'd reconsidered and didn't want me to go away. That didn't happen.

"You're going to have so much fun," he said, holding both my hands as we stood across from each other.

GIVE ME A 38!

"Yeah, I know, I can't wait."

I did my best not to show that I was a little disappointed by his nonchalant attitude. I know that he isn't exactly **HAPPY** I am going away. He just genuinely wants me to have a good time. But I think I wanted Bevan to be like, "Nooooooo! Don't go!!!!!" and beg me on his knees to stay. Ooh! Or to do a little cheer like, "Oh Maddy, When You're Gone I Go Batty!"

Not that I would listen. I just wanted to hear how much he was going to miss me. Tears would have been a nice touch. Ok fine, that's a little extreme, but what I'm saying is, even though I don't really **WANT** to feel guilty about leaving him, it would have been nice if he gave me a little bit of a harder time about it. I can't help but think about Evan's reaction to my going—and how even though it's annoying to be given a guilt trip, it's nice to feel missed. Is it weird that my best guy friend doesn't want me to leave, but my boyfriend is all for me leaving? Something is wrong with this picture. . . .

GIVE ME A 39!

Bevan did do something cute, though: Right before I turned to go inside, he handed me a note, folded into a tiny square. "Don't read it until you're on the plane," he said seriously.

"Why? Is there a secret message in there?" I asked.

"No." He smiled. "It's the rule about plane letters. You can't read them until you're actually on the plane."

"Ooookay," I said, smiling back. "Talk to you soon."

"Yep. Bye," he said, before turning back to go to his mom's car.

"Hey!" I called out after him. "Happy New Year!"

"Happy New Year, Mads."

Now it's time to go sit in front of the tube, eat lots of hors d'oeuvres off fancy plates, and welcome in the New Year with Mom.

We even bought those dorky party hats and some kazoos so we can cheer when the ball drops. All in all, a perfectly acceptable send-off day for my trip. Woohoo!!

GIVE ME A 40!

Sunday, January 1

Morning, up in the air—FOREVER!!

Holiday Spirit Level:

Cheering in the New Year

Seriously, what is it with airplane movies? Do they purposely choose the saddest ones because the stewardesses get a kick out of making passengers cry? I just watched what must have been a straight-to-DVD movie about a guy and his loyal canine friend. The guy dies and the dog waits for him at the train station for years, hoping he'll come out of the station door. I seriously went through a whole mini pack of tissues by the end of it.

And now I'm in a melancholy mood.

For some reason (maybe it's because I'm not being distracted by a dumb airplane movie right now), I can't stop thinking about the way Evan acted when I was at his house the other day after I told him I was going away. It was like we'd never see each other again. Drama queen much? C'mon, it's only a week! Which I

GIVE ME A 4!!

guess is long for, like, Evan and Maddy time (at least in the old days). But it's not like I up and go on fantastic vacations to New York all that often.

Wait. Total flashback happening. What was that **INSANE** thing that Katie said to me on the bus back from the Regional Qualifier? That Evan has the hots for **MOI**!! How did I forget about that comment until now? Could **THAT** be why he acted so weird and why he's so upset that I'm leaving? No. There's not a chance Katie was serious. And even if she was, she must have had her information waaayyyy wrong. There's just no way he feels like that about **ME**. We've been friends since we were five. We built pillow fortresses together. I mean, it just wouldn't make sense. I don't even know why I'm considering the possibility. Because the chances of me and Evan getting together? Almost as impossible as me finding a comfortable position in this dumb seat on the plane. Ouch.

Anyway, after the awful/sappy movie (and the super-sappy Evan thoughts), I put on my iPod and vegged out for a bit. When I opened my eyes, the stewardess was centimeters away from my face. I nearly jumped out of my seat—but obvs couldn't exactly jump (thanks to my seat belt and TSA regulations!).

"Miss, would you like another 7UP?" asked the

GIVE ME A 42!

stewardess. Her breath smelled like tomato juice. Guess she'd been sampling some of the airplane's stock. PS-I **HATE** tomato juice.

YUCK!

"Um, sure," I said. One reason I hate flying is that every two minutes someone is asking you to either get up, sit down, drink something, eat something, or listen to someone scare the pants off you because of reported turbulence. But my biggest flying peeve is that I am always so sore from practice and yet I can't stretch out without picking someone else's nose by accident.

This is something Dad and Beth don't really have to worry about, because Miss Fancy Flier has so many miles from all her business trips she scored them seats in first class.

Mom was actually annoyed when I told her about me sitting in coach. She said, "Why should you be treated like a second-class citizen while they travel like celebrities?" I didn't really care, and I knew Mom was just annoyed that Dad never did things like travel first class when they were married. And I know them sitting

GIVE ME A 43!

there and me sitting here isn't anything personal.

But I was curious.

So I decided to wander over to where my dad was sitting. When I got to the curtain that separated first class from the rest of us, one of the stewardesses was like, "Excuse me, miss, but is your seat here?"

"Uh, um, no," I stuttered. "But my dad is sitting here, and I need to tell him something."

"The first class area is for first class only," she said, as if she were reading from a manual.

"Yes, but I need to tell him something important."

Ok, so that was a lie, but just a tiny one.

She grimaced as if the thought of allowing me through put her in great pain. Then finally she nodded her head to tell me it was all right for me to pass. Guess she was bending Ye Olde Airplane Rules in a major way and didn't want anyone to know she approved of my trespassing.

Dad and Beth were sipping cappuccinos and reading their magazines when I came up to them. I don't know how people do that. I just can't concentrate on reading when I'm on a plane. I always think I'll do homework, or read a magazine, but I get so antsy two minutes into it. But Dad and Beth looked pretty absorbed in their mags.

I tapped Dad on the shoulder.

GIVE ME A 44!

"Oh, hi, hon," he said, removing his glasses. "How you doing back there?"

"I'm surviving," I said, with a shrug.

"You teaching the other passengers some killer cheer moves?"

"Please don't say 'killer.' Hey, did you get any cookies or anything?"

Dad smiled. "Indeed I did," he said, unwrapping a chocolate chip cookie from a linen airplane napkin.

"Awesome," I said, taking a bite. Mmmm. Still warm.

I crouched down as close to his seat as possible so as not to disturb the other passengers with my non-first-class presence.

"So, Dad, I was wondering—is our hotel anywhere near Times Square?" I was hoping it was, because I know that's where all the Broadway shows are. And even better, it's not that far a walk to the Garment District—at least that is what Wikipedia said.

"We're staying at a boutique hotel that Beth likes on the Upper West Side of Manhattan. It's quite a walk from Times Square." He cast Beth an adoring look. "But you know how much Beth and I love to walk."

That's funny. He used to hate walking anywhere when I was a kid. He'd take a car to go to our next-door neighbor's house. Hmm. Walking in the icy

GIVE ME A 45!

cold winter air—not exactly my idea of a good time. Isn't New York famous for its taxicabs?

Then I remembered the list of things to do in New York that Bevan had given me, and there were a few fun-sounding things on the Upper West Side. Like a flea market that sells cool vintage accessories and clothes and is always open no matter how cold it is. I'll have to tell Dad I have some ideas of my own about what we should do this week.

"Madison, would you care for my pillow?" asked Beth. Ok, so that was kind of nice of her. I probably should have said, "No, gracias," because I'm sure she was just offering it to impress my dad, and deep down would have liked to keep her special pillow. But the part of me that was like, "Yay! Now I'll have a slightly less awful flight!" took it anyway.

I squeezed past a bunch of people whose legs were taking up half the aisles. I'm just grateful that my seat partner is a tiny old lady who takes up only about half her seat. She's clearly a bit strange, but at least I can breathe sitting next to her. The only annoying thing is that the old lady brought her cat with her on the plane and keeps talking to it the whole ride. But since the cat has to be stowed in its carry case under the seat, it looks like she's just talking to the

GIVE ME A 46!

floor whenever she leans down
to say hi to the cat. Every two
minutes she's like, "Here, kitty,
kitty! Mommy loves you! Do you
love Mommy?" And then her cat
gives a loud "Meow!" back to
her. Then she looks over
at me and smiles, like I
should recognize the brilliance
of her cat being able to have
conversations with humans. I've

given in and smiled back at her at least five times in a
row, to be polite, but after the tenth time, I decided
it's time to pretend not to hear her.

   At one point I was so bored I was about to count my
split ends—and then I remembered!! Bevan's note.

   It was crumpled into one of the little pockets
on the inside of my backpack—I guess where you're
supposed to keep secret things like your ID and keys
and stuff like that. On the back of it, it said, "For Your
Plane-Reading Pleasure Only! No Peeking!" Wow, he was
really serious about these plane letter rules.

   I unfolded it and smoothed it out against my jeans.

   Dear Maddy, by the time you read this you'll be on
your way to your cool vacay (hey, that rhymes). If it

snows in New York, take pics! There's nothing like the big city covered in snow. Especially Central Park. Don't let your dad or Beth annoy you too much, and make sure you see some of the things on the list I gave you. You won't be disappointed. I'll be missing you.—B.

I feel a little better now ☺.

And if you looked really closely, you could see a teeny, tiny circular stain . . . a teardrop, perhaps???

GIVE ME A 48!

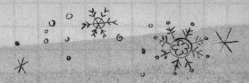

Monday, January 2

Morning, in an itsy-bitsy teeny-weeny ... hotel

Spirit Level:

Feeling Merry and Bright

When we got to the hotel last night, I was so tired I was barely able to register what the place looked like. I felt like a zombie. I guess I needed a rest after all the insane workouts we've been doing with the Grizzlies.

I think I just collapsed onto the comfy mattress, threw the thick comforter over my head, and fell asleep right away. Didn't even brush my teeth. Yuck.

NEEEED... BEEED... NOOOW...

But I just woke up, and now that I'm actually looking around, I'm realizing what they say about New York hotels is true:

GIVE ME A 49!

This room is as small as my bathroom at home. It is crazy! I mean, it's pretty and everything—but basically all I have is this big ol' bed in here and a shelf with a TV on it, and that's practically it. Whoever designed this room must have been thinking stick figures would do really well living here. T.G. I am not sharing a room with Dad and Beth. Talk about too close for comfort. At least I have my own bathroom.

But still, I can't really complain. My own hotel room! How cool is that? I've never had a hotel room all to myself before. The walls are covered in this old-fashioned wallpaper that has a swirly flower pattern, and my window has long, velvety, floor-length drapes the color of wine. I feel like I'm inside an antique dollhouse.

Once I realized that there was no closet, I squeezed all my stuff into the thimble-size dresser. Then I started to get pretty antsy, so I tried to do some exercises. There's no way I'm going to let myself get totally out of shape while every other cheerleader is working twice as hard this week. But it IS going to be hard to practice real cheer stuff in here when I can barely lift my leg without hitting the door. Too bad this hotel doesn't have a gym. But I guess anything is better than nothing.

I took the tiny chair that was in the corner and

GIVE ME A
50!

propped it so the back was against the bed. It was just right for doing some triceps dips. Then I lay on the floor (I know, kind of gross—who knows how old this carpet is?) and did some major sit-ups until the phone rang.

"Hey, Mads, you ready?" said Dad in his chipper morning voice.

"I haven't even showered yet."

"Well, get dressed, sleepyhead. We're going to explore the neighborhood."

"Twenty minutes?"

"Yep."

I'm not exactly the fastest person in the world when it comes to getting ready (also, I had to write my first New York City journal entry). I rifled through my drawer and tried to put together an outfit that said, "So Not a Tourist." No Hawaiian shirts and camcorders for me! Blech.

GIVE ME A 5!!

I opted for a baby-doll dress with little flower buds on it, and layered a chunky cable-knit cardigan over it. Then I put on some heavy-knit tights (fashionable AND practical!) and my favorite walking boots. Perfection (if I do say so myself)!

Ok, so I'm about to go check out this place. More later!

GIVE ME A 52!

NIGHT, HOTEL LIBRARY

First of all, I like this part of New York a lot. Dad, Beth, and I wandered around near our hotel all day today, and it was so much fun. We went to this little café that was in one of my dad's favorite movies. He said the movie was about a woman who writes to this guy and becomes pen pals with him, until they finally meet and she realizes the guy she'd been writing to is this guy she can't stand. Anyway, the café was so pretty, with all these French paintings on the walls. (Beth told me that they were by a guy named Toulouse-Lautrec.) I ordered the "New York Brunch" because, hey! I'm in New York. The plate came arranged so cutely: a bagel, cream cheese, tomatoes, capers, lettuce, and smoked salmon. I, like, completely inhaled it. See, I'm a New Yorker already ☺. Even though I was stuffed, Beth insisted that we try a couple of their famous desserts. My **FAVE** was their angel food cake. So soft and fluffy!

Afterward we wandered through the flea market that Bevan told me about. There were so many cool crafts, jewelry, and clothes. Score! Presents for everyone!! I found this bracelet that Lanie would die for because they're made of leather and have charms hanging from them that are all "dark" kind of things.

GIVE ME A 53!

Lanie's new bracelet skulls, and snakes, and stuff like that. (At least the Lanie I USED to know will love it. . . .)

And I found a dress that would be great for the spring.

Beth and Dad hung around the antique furniture, trying to decide on a side table for their living room. Bor-ing. I found a food stand that sold DELISH hot chocolate, so I took a pic and posted it on Evan's Facebook wall.

"The holiday hot chocolate tradition continues!" I wrote.

I hope he'll think it's funny (and write back to me soon).

Then I texted Lanes to tell her about her prezzie.

"Just found the perf thing—U R so going to heart it. That is if Dustin hasn't turned you."

"Ha-ha. Thnx! Ur the bestest."

"Oh, stop," I wrote.

"So guess what? One more day till I C my luvvvv!"

"Lanes! Remember, he's just a celeb. He has to be sweet to all his fans."

"U never kno," wrote Lanie. "When he meets me, he

GIVE ME A 54!

mite fall in luv. Do u doubt my charms?"

"No, no doubt here. Keep hope alive!"

I put my phone in my pocket and took a deep breath. Lanie's gone off the deep end with this Dustin thing. I bet if I looked into her eyes right now I'd see those pinwheels that they show in cartoons when a character goes nutso. At least it's only one more day until she meets him face-to-face. I can only hope that then she'll realize he's not even that cute in person or something. Or maybe he'll have a booger in his nose while he's signing her book.

Please, please, please let something happen to snap her back to normal. Then her room can go back to the way it used to be with posters of weird art and intellectual quotes on her wall and all her old books everywhere.

For dinner we went to an Ethiopian restaurant nearby. I was not so thrilled with the idea at first. I even considered running out of the hotel to grab a hot dog on the street so that I wouldn't have to eat the Ethiopian food. But it actually wasn't as weird as I thought. I'd never had that kind of food before, but since I'm on vacation, I thought, I might as well be adventurous. Even though that didn't really work out the last time I went to a restaurant with Beth and Dad

GIVE ME A 55!

(the time I like to call "the Great Foie Gras Disaster").

The waiter led us to a table, and to my surprise, we were seated right on the floor. That's right. As in no chairs to sit on. It kind of felt like we were at one of those theme restaurants in Disneyland where everything is supposed to be "authentic." Beth ordered a bunch of dishes whose names gave no hint as to what might be inside them.

"Aren't you excited, Mads?" asked Dad. "You've never eaten Ethiopian before."

"Oh, have you?" I asked.

Dad looked a little sheepish. "No, but I'm very much looking forward to it," he said with as much enthusiasm as possible.

When the food came, Beth showed us how to tear small pieces off the large piece of bread that had been placed in the center of the table and scoop things up with them. Everything was MUCHO spicy, but the bread and rice helped. I even got to eat with my hands without Dad making some kind of comment about my manners. The restaurant didn't even give us forks, since the real way to eat the food is to scoop it up onto your bread. Never in my wildest dreams did I ever imagine a scenario where eating food with silverware would be considered rude. Cool, huh?

GIVE ME A 56!

The thing is, Dad usually makes annoying comments when Beth's around. But he's actually been really fun so far—maybe it's the New York air? Maybe it's because Beth has been in the best mood ever?

Either way? I like this less picky version of Dad. I only hope it lasts.

GIVE ME A 57!

Spirit Level:

More Like "Holiday Drama"

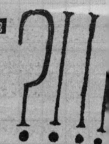

OMG, drama is **SOOOO** needy. It's like having my little sister's totally annoying, dorky best friend following me **ALL** over the place **ALL** the time!! I mean, if I had a little sister, which I don't. Still, the point is I can't believe drama needed to follow me all the way to New York City. I've been here, like, all of five minutes.

Ok, here's the deal. This morning we were all ready to leave for the day when Beth decided she needed her **CASHMERE** gloves instead of her **WOOL** ones.

"I won't be a minute," she said, as she bounded up the stairs back to their room.

I plopped down on the hotel couch, ready to kill some time with Dad. But then I saw that Beth was looking back down at us, as if she wanted Dad to follow her.

GIVE ME A 58!

"Well," he sighed. "I guess I should go up too. The ol'
ball and chain must need something from me."

Ooookay, weird. I can be in a hotel room all by
myself, but Beth can't go up to hers alone to get a pair
of gloves?

Whatever. So I was sitting there, scrolling through
my messages, when someone walked past me, leaving
behind a cloud of perfume that smelled unmistakably
familiar. It was the almost sickly sweet smell of
coconut and strawberries that I only know one person
to wear: the one, the only, Katie Parker. At first I
was like, "Wow, Mads, someone has cheer withdrawal."
But when I looked up, I could not believe my eyes.
The girl who left the trail of Eau de Katie looked
EXACTLY like Katie Parker from behind: Blond hair
in the signature Katie high ponytail—the one she always
wears during cheer practice. The same plaid winter
jacket Katie's been sporting since it got cold. (Yeah,
I know I sound like a stalker, but it's totally my job
to keep tabs on the Titans—especially their captain.) I
ran after the girl to get a better look, but the bellboy
blocked my way when I got to the door. Didn't he know
I was in super sleuth mode? I scrambled around him and
burst through the door, but I was too late. She had
disappeared around the corner by then.

GIVE ME A
59!

What was taking Dad and Beth so long? I wanted to get out there and find her so I could make sure it wasn't Katie. But Dad has a thing against me walking around by myself, and he would have totally freaked out if he came downstairs to find me out and about on my own. So instead I sat back down in the couch and fidgeted, too hyper to read a magazine from the coffee table.

As I sat there, I thought about how there was no way Katie Parker could be in New York too. She of all people wouldn't miss winter break cheer practice—or ANY practice, for that matter. In fact, I don't think she even missed practice when she had the awful stomach bug that was going around a few weeks ago—that's what I call devotion. Also, what would the chances be of her being not only here in New York, but also in this very same hotel? The cheer gods couldn't be THAT mean.

I texted Jacqs to tell her the funny story.

"Get this: A Katie P. twin has followed me allll the way to NYC. I swear, this girl looks exactly like her, and she is in my hotel. Random, rite?"

My phone rang two seconds later. I looked down: It was Jacqui.

"Got your message," Jacqui said over the noise of

GIVE ME A GO!

cars honking and people yelling. She must be either at the mall parking lot, I thought, or in the middle of the highway.

"How crazy is that?" I said.

"Maybe not so crazy," she said. "I have to go in a sec, but I wanted to tell you that Katie actually wasn't at practice yesterday."

"Ohmigod, seriously?" I asked. This had to be some kind of crazy coincidence.

"I thought she was sick or something, but then I asked Hilary, and she said Katie went on a last-minute trip to her grandparents' house in Wisconsin."

"You're joking," I said.

"Nope. And the Titans were kind of annoyed, but Katie told them she didn't have a choice."

"So weird," I said. "Do you really think it's her? Seriously, why would she even be in New York City?"

"I don't know," said Jacqui. "Do you really think she'd lie to her team? That's pretty shady."

"Mads?" My dad was shouting to me from the top of the stairs because he couldn't see me from his view on the landing. "You still down there?"

I put my hand over the speaker to shout back at him. "Yes, just on the phone!"

"Ok, Jacqs, I gotta go too. I'll keep you posted."

GIVE ME A
6!!

As soon as I hung up the phone, it hit me: what if this "twin" actually IS Katie Parker?

AFTERNOON, FOXWOODS THEATRE

This afternoon we walked to Times Square to see if we could nab some cheap tix to a Broadway show. I was down for seeing almost anything—just to be able to say I went to one. And of course, if I didn't, Jared would strangle me. I was secretly hoping we'd get to see Wicked, since Jared has made us all listen to the sound track a million times. He's completely obsessed with Kristin Chenoweth—and loves singing her solos when we're doing laps around the gym. It's become kind of an anthem for our practices.

GIVE ME A 62!

Anyway, we were walking down Broadway, and I saw that familiar blond head again. It was the Katie Twin, walking with some woman (her mom, maybe?). I mean, I saw her from far away, but the more I looked at the back of her head, the more I realized that not only did she have the same hairstyle as Katie, her head was even the same shape as Katie's (yes, I know the shape of Katie's head. It's sad but not really important now. . . .). I started picking up my pace so we could catch up with her.

"Maddy, what's the rush?" asked Dad, jogging up to me.

"Oh, nothing, Dad," I said, picking up my walk/sprint even more. "Just decided that I uh, need a little exercise after being cooped up in that tiny hotel room."

We must have looked pretty funny dressed in full winter gear, speed walking down Broadway. Just when I caught up with the Twin, I slowed down a bit. If it wasn't her, I didn't want it to be completely obvious that I was checking her out like a weirdo. And if it was her, well, what would I

Katie's twin!

GIVE ME A 63!

say, exactly? To my relief, I finally saw that the girl was wearing a very un-Katie outfit: leg warmers and extra-baggy sweatpants, from what I could see. Kind of like a dancer.

I finally slowed down and caught my breath. Katie would never be caught dead wearing something like that. She's all cheer all the time. Even when she's wearing jeans and a T-shirt, it's always tight jeans and a tight T-shirt. I've never seen her wear sweatpants—even during practice. "There's no way that's Katie," I said out loud without meaning to.

"Who, honey?" asked Dad.

"Oh, nothing. I just saw a girl who looked like Marcia Brady."

Dad and Beth exchanged a look like "kids these days."

"All right, sweetie," said Dad.

We kept walking, and all I could think was wow, I really hope that isn't actually Katie Parker. I mean, she and I have been ok with each other since our showdown at the Regional Qualifier, but there's still some tension there. And I didn't exactly **NEED** her staying in my hotel—during my **VACATION**. Can't a girl get a break?

So the Katie Twin and the woman next to her

GIVE ME A
64!

started slowing down their pace and pulled out a map. The woman pointed to a huge building nearby, and the Katie Twin was definitely yelling at her. I picked up my collar so they wouldn't see us walking right past them, but I decided to sneak one more good look to make extra sure. And that's when I was thrown into Obviousville, Population 2.

There was no mistaking it. This was no twin. It was the Real Katie.

I must have looked like I'd seen a ghost, because Dad was like, "Are you ok?"

"Oh, just great!" I said. "Just, um . . . saw someone I know, that's all."

"What a small world! You want to go say hi?" said Dad. Beth nodded encouragingly. "We'll wait."

I literally grabbed his arm and pulled us all away from the scene of the crime. "Oh, no, it's cool! You know, I really could use a bathroom. Can we hurry up?"

I needed us to walk as far away as possible from Katie Parker. I didn't want her to see me just yet.

Obviously she lied about Wisconsin. How is she going to explain that? And what is she doing dressed in dancer's clothes? I can't put the pieces together. I need to think about things before running up to her and being like, "Hey, you!"

GIVE ME A
65!

We ended up getting last-minute tickets to Spider-Man on Broadway. And the seats are pretty good! It's intermission right now, and the show so far has been absolutely insane! I'm glad it's taken my mind off the Katie thing a little bit. **OH**, and the actor playing Spidey is kind of dreamy. The acrobatics are so cool—the actors are literally flying over our heads. I'm wondering now, how I could incorporate Spider-Man-like moves into one of our routines.

You never know where inspiration will strike, huh?

LATER TONIGHT, IN THE ROOM O' DOOM (JUST KIDDING)

So, this afternoon while Beth and Dad were napping in their room, I went on video chat to say hi to whoever was online. I'm actually really starting to dig this little room o' mine. It's so cozy when it's dark out, and the glow of my monitor is reflected in the floor-to-ceiling window. I was hoping to have a chance to tell Lanie what had happened earlier today. Luckily, she was online. And guess what? She actually gave me an entire **TWO MINUTES** to talk about something that was **NOT** Dustin related. Imagine ☺. I'm pretty proud of her, considering how obsessed

GIVE ME A 66!

she's been with him lately. Unfortunately, when I saw her room in the background of the screen, I didn't notice anything different. It still looks like a Dustin Barker extravaganza in there. I told Lanie about my Katie sightings and how now I am absolutely sure that it's her, and not a Bizarro Katie look-alike. At first Lanie was like, "You sure you're not making this up to distract me from the Dustin thing?"

"No, Lanes. I actually do have other things going on separate from worrying about your love life."

"I know, I know," Lanie said, taking a small section of her hair and making it into a tiny braid. "But your story is so crazy I could have sworn you made it up."

"Yeah, it is crazy. And unfortunately, it's 100% true."

"Gee, Mads, I'm sorry. This week was supposed to be a vacation. Not Part III in the Katie Parker saga," she said, putting both hands over her heart. "So . . . are you going to talk to her?"

"Ha!" I said. "More like hide from her. The last time the two of us had a conversation, it was about the whole me and Bevan thing. I know she doesn't completely hate me anymore, but I'm sure I'm not her first choice in vacation buddies—and she's obviously not mine."

Lanie nodded her head in agreement, and I could see

GIVE ME A 67!

her brows furrow the way they do when she's worried about me. When it comes to any of the Titans, Lanie keeps a safe distance. They really freaked out last month when she did that article for the Daily Angeles— the one about cheerleaders getting more funding from the school than other teams. And even though the article ended up saying tons of great things about the Titans—like how they kick so much butt that they deserve all the moola they get—some Titans were still miffed. Some of the girls felt like Lanie had given out some of the insider secrets she learned from all her interviews with them. I know that she didn't say anything wrong, but you can't win with those girls.

"Maybe you should get a wig so she won't recognize you," Lanie suggested.

"Or maybe I can just hide in my hotel room until the week is over."

"Ok, good luck with that," said Lanie.

After I said good-bye to Lanes, I went onto chat to say a quick hello to Evan, but SURPRISE, SURPRISE, he didn't write back. He's usually online all hours at night—it even said he was "active" on the chat screen. I figure (or hope) he just left his desk for a second—but still. Annoying! He could have written to ME, right? The entire time I've been here he hasn't

GIVE ME A 68!

sent me a single text or e-mail—not even a post on my Facebook wall, even though I posted something funny on his yesterday. I remember when we used to chat and text a million times a day. It's like he's giving me the silent treatment for having left Port Angeles for a week. But not contacting me just because I can't participate in our usual winter break tradition this year is sooooo immature. And Evan's not really like that—not usually. Grrrr. What **IS** his problem?

Anyway, Jacqui **WAS** online, and I was dying to tell her about the Real Katie sighting. But I could tell as soon as she came onto the video screen that something was up. She had that "look."

"So you won't believe this," said Jacqui.

"Dish," I said, settling into the desk chair. I always like a good piece of gossip.

"It's not good," she said, shaking her head.

Oh, boy.

"So, right before practice, Ms. Burger gave me some random piece of paper to give to Coach Carolyn because she had to leave before Coach got there. And I knew I wasn't supposed to peek, but . . ." Jacqui started playing with her curls the way she usually does when she's anxious.

"But?" I asked, dying with anticipation.

GIVE ME A 69!

"I couldn't help it. I peeked! And I saw what it said on it," Jacqui said, blushing a little. "I was worried, you know? The paper looked all 'official.'"

I was beginning to lose my patience. "Just spill the beans, Jacqs."

Turns out it was a note from the headquarters of the Get Up and Cheer board. The board in charge of the competition we've been training so hardcore for—our only reason for cheering at this moment in time. Yup, that one. Everyone on the squad is looking forward to it—it's practically all we talk about in the locker rooms lately. Unfortunately, this little note was **NOT** a love note telling us how awesome and amazing the Grizzlies are. Nope. Whoever runs the competition wrote to Ms. Burger and Mom to tell them that our squad is going to be rejected from the competition because of our **GRADES**. Um, yeah. Major freak-out straight ahead.

"What are you talking about? I thought everyone has a B or above average," I said. Then I thought about Ian and Matt, and how they've been known to skip a class or two. But not lately—they've definitely been upping the ante since becoming more serious about cheer. "Even Ian and Matt have been keeping their grades up."

GIVE ME A 70!

"It's not Ian and Matt," she said, shaking her head. "It's . . . Katarina."

What?!? Katarina? She is superserious about studying and is always talking about how much homework she has. She hardly comes to our squad dinners anymore because she wants to be "serious to the schoolwork."

"Um, please explain pronto. I'm, like, not comprendo-ing here," I said.

"I was shocked too," said Jacqui. "But the note said that she has a C. Each squad member has to have at least a B- in every class in order for the squad to qualify."

"Yikes. So then what did you do? Did you talk to Katarina?"

Jacqui bit her lip. "I gave the note to Coach first, and I guess after practice she told Katarina what the deal is. Katarina came hysterically crying to me. She was like, 'It's the social studies! I fail at being the social!' But I couldn't even laugh, because you know this, like, directly affects us. She told me she hasn't been doing well this whole time but was too embarrassed to tell anyone on the team. Mrs. Tuttle has even been giving her extra help, but it's still not working. And now she feels like this is all her fault."

GIVE ME A 7!!

"Wow," I said, taking this all in. "This is awful."

If we miss out on going to this competition, I can't even imagine how the squad will feel. The Grizzlies need this, especially after going to the Regional Qualifier and only being able to watch from the sidelines while more advanced teams like the Titans tore up the mats.

"It's worse than awful," continued Jacqui. "Katarina said that Mrs. Tuttle and her parents say she might have to quit cheerleading if she doesn't up her grade. They think cheer is taking away from her studies."

"Ohmigod! We'll be ruined!"

"Yeah. I promised her I'd think of something," said Jacqui. "But I have no idea what. And there's a big test coming up right after break, too."

That's when I remembered: "Hey, isn't Tabitha Sue some kind of history genius? And Matt's, like, scary good at memorizing stuff. Maybe he could teach Katarina some tricks."

Jacqui smiled, looking relieved. "I knew you'd have an idea," she said happily.

"Let's have an emergency meeting tomorrow with the squad. Just video chat me in. We'll tell the team what's going on and ask everyone to pitch in however they can to help Katarina ace this next test."

"Well, it is winter break. People have a lot of free

GIVE ME A 72!

time on their hands," said Jacqui.

"Yeah, and if we can get her to do really well on this next test, maybe she can turn her grade around and we can still be in the competition. Then she wouldn't have to leave the team."

"She'll have to get an A on this test to pull her grade in that class up to a B-," grumbled Jacqui.

It's so unfair-Katarina tries so hard to do well in school and in cheer. It's not like she's a slacker.

"Maybe someone can talk to Mrs. Tuttle and ask her to go a little easier on her?" (Guess New York is making me into a "glass half full" kind of gal.)

"Yeah, good luck," said Jacqui with a smile. "Mrs. T. doesn't look like someone who lies awake at night worrying about cheerleaders' grades."

Jacqui had a point.

I heard someone call to Jacqui from another room. "Ok, gotta run," she said. "We're having a family cookie bake-off."

"Uh, a what?"

"Don't ask. Talk to ya later."

After that news I was really hoping someone would lift my spirits. I knew it wasn't going to be Evan . . . and Bevan wasn't online either. But he did write me an e-mail—probably the shortest e-mail known to man—but an e-mail nonetheless: Hope the big city is treatin' u well!

I haven't been worrying about Bevan being out of touch as much as I have been thinking about Evan (again, something's wrong with that picture . . .), but I have to admit the shortness of his e-mail is making me start to wonder. Does he just not miss me? What is it with the boys in my life? Are they all at some superfun Forget Maddy party together?

Still, I'm more upset about E. I must be going craaaazy.

GIVE ME A 74!

Ok, so I've seen the New York City subways in movies, like, a billion times, but I still didn't expect it to be **THIS** crowded. My face was stuck in someone's armpit for, like, ten minutes before I got this seat. Delish!

T.G. it's freezing outside— people are nice and covered up, so I was saved by the enormous puffy coat that separated said armpit from my nose.

Anyway, I woke up this morning from the rattle of

GIVE ME A 75!

my cell against the night table. It was a text from Jacqui:

"Don't 4get, 3:45 today, Grizzly mtg."

I looked out the window: another crisp, cold day. The sky was so clear and blue it almost hurt to look at it. I showered, used my curling iron to create some extra waves in my hair, then picked out New York Outfit Numero 2: stretch pants with a skirt (one of my own creations) over them, a slouchy sweater, and ankle boots. I'd seen someone on the street sporting a similar look yesterday, which gave me the idea.

wink!

Dad called my room to say we were going to go to a special place for pastries (he and Beth supposedly both love eating there whenever they come to New York), so I shouldn't worry about missing breakfast at the hotel. Which for

my awesome outfit!

GIVE ME A 76!

some stupid reason is super-duper early. Who wakes up at five a.m. with a giant hankering for Special K?

I hung out in the lobby for a few minutes, reading the mini version of the paper that they have lying on all the little side tables. I love anything mini—even if it's world news. I plopped down in a comfy armchair and started reading the sports section, when I heard an oh-so-familiar voice.

"Mom! Come on! We're going to be late for my class."

I looked up from my paper, hoping that it wasn't who I thought it was (even though I totally knew it was EXACTLY who I thought it was). There is no ignoring this problem away. I still can't believe it. Of all the hotels in New York City, she has to be in mine! What, was there an article in Wake Up, Port Angeles telling people they should all go to this one hotel when they're in NYC?

She saw me as soon as she reached the bottom of the stairs. A surprised "oh" escaped her lips as we locked eyes.

Neither of us said anything for what seemed like eons. Finally, because it was mega awkward, I caved.

"Hey, Katie," I said, because . . . what else was I going to do? Ignore her?

THIS did not look good: Two cheerleading captains

GIVE ME A 7?!

playing hooky from their responsibilities back home? I was pretty sure she felt guilty about not being with the Titans over break, because her face immediately got all red.

"Um. Uh. Hey!" she said, as she walked toward me. She was playing with the zipper on her jacket awkwardly. I put down my paper and looked up at her. I noticed her mom had come downstairs too, looking unhappy about something. Katie appeared to ignore her, though.

"So, uh, what are you doing here?" she asked me.

I decided to stand, because it felt awkward having her stand over me like that.

"My dad asked me to come with him and his girlfriend for a little vacation," I explained. "And it's kind of a once-in-a-lifetime opportunity." I don't know why, but at that moment I actually felt nervous too. It wasn't like I had lied to my team about where I was going. Like SOME people (ahem, cough, cough).

Katie picked at a cuticle and looked back at her mom, who was now talking to the front desk person. "I'm sort of in a similar sitch," she said.

"You mean, your parents made you come with them on a vacation too? I thought you were supposed to be in Wisconsin."

GIVE ME A
78!

"How did you . . .?" she broke off, suddenly looking at me all suspiciously, like I read her diary or something.

"Jacqui told me. Hilary told her," I explained.

"Oh. Wow. Didn't realize my winter break activities were, like, news or something."

Katie took a seat on the arm of the chair I'd been sitting on, so I sat back down across from her.

"Everything's news at Port Angeles."

"True," she agreed. "Hey, can you do me a solid?"

Ummm. Why was Katie asking ME to do HER a favor? We aren't friends.

"Could you, like, maybe try not to tell anyone back home that you saw me here? I can't let this get back to the team. Not even Clementine or Hilary," she said guiltily.

Oops. Too late! I knew Lanie was good to keep a secret, though.

"I won't say anything, but do you plan on telling me why you're really here?" I raised my eyebrow, waiting for an explanation. It must have been pretty bad if she was lying to her team—and even her best friends—about it. Maybe Katie had committed a terrible crime and was getting some kind of major surgery so she could create a whole new identity. Or maybe the people in her family were some kind of secret agents who traveled

GIVE ME A 79!

the world collecting clues, and Katie had to go with them?

Hmm. No, that wouldn't explain why she was wearing that weird outfit yesterday. Katie looked left to right, like she was worried her conversation with me was being filmed. Finally, she leaned forward on the chair and spilled the beans. "Ok, fine. I was never going to my grandparents' house in Wisconsin. I lied, but I swear I have a good reason," she said, crossing her arms over her chest.

Katie Parker: Secret Agent

Just then I noticed that she was wearing a getup similar to the one she'd worn yesterday—with all that dance gear. She was in full-out Dance Pants mode: baggy pants over tights, a leotard, and leg warmers. I couldn't imagine she was going to a cheer clinic dressed like that. Something was definitely up.

"You ready, honey?" asked her mom, putting her hand on Katie's shoulder. I saw Katie jump a little out of her seat.

"Mom, you scared me. Don't sneak up on me like that."

Her mom let out an exasperated sigh. "You made me rush to get ready so we could go to this dance

GIVE ME AN 80!

studio, and now I'm waiting for you?" Her voice sounded annoyed.

"Mom!" Katie said loudly. "This is Madison. From school—she's on the Grizzly squad." She nudged her head in my direction so her mom would notice me. Katie had emphasized the word "Grizzly" like she wanted her mom to know she was talking to a fellow cheerleader. Or to a loser. Hard to tell.

"Nice to meet you," said Mrs. Parker as she shook my hand. "Katiebug, I'm going to call your dad—meet me outside when you're ready." She put on a pair of long red gloves. "But we're going to be late if you don't hurry," she chided, before turning away.

"Nice meeting you!" I shouted after her. Then I turned back to Katie. "Katiebug?" I asked, smirking.

"Oh, whatever," she said, flushing a little.

"So . . . is this a cheer audition?" I couldn't help but ask, even though I had a feeling it wasn't.

"Well, kind of," she said, averting her eyes. "It's, um, this new type of dance thing for cheerleaders."

"What do you mean?" I asked.

"You, uh, have to be selected. I couldn't tell anyone, but it's a special class that teaches captains elite dance moves." She tried to smile, but I could see she was faking it.

GIVE ME AN 8!!

"Well, I'm a captain," I pointed out. "Maybe I should give it a try?"

Finally Katie sighed and threw her hands up in the air. I could tell that at this point she'd given up trying to lie. "All right. This is a huge secret, but the reason I'm here is that there is an audition for a performing arts school I really want to go to. It's a dance audition."

It all made sense at that moment—the fact that she had kept this trip a secret from everyone, her clothes, her embarrassment at seeing me.

"So, when you say 'dance,' you don't mean cheer dance, I assume?"

Katie shook her head no, almost apologetically. "No, like dance dance." She put her hands over her head like a ballerina about to twirl.

Suddenly my face gave her this look, similar to the look I would have given Lanie if she'd just told me Dustin Barker wanted to marry her.

Even though I knew Katie was up to something secretive, I never would have guessed that it was something like this. I've never known Katie as wanting to be anything other than the best cheerleader in the world. That was always her thing. But I guess I was wrong.

"Dance is my passion," said Katie, after registering

GIVE ME AN 82!

the shock on my face. "No one at school knows, but it always has been. I got into cheer because it had a lot of dance in it and I liked the challenge. Even after I joined the Titans, I never thought I wouldn't be able to do both. But no matter how hard I tried, I just couldn't keep up with my dance classes. And especially after becoming captain, I hardly ever get to go to class. Practice and competitions have practically taken over my life."

"Sorry, it's taking me a little time to process all this. I've never even heard of you being a dancer," I said incredulously.

Katie smiled. "I had to keep it on the DL," she explained. "I knew that people wouldn't consider me a serious captain if I was spending all my spare time doing something else. I mean, you know what it's like, right?"

I nodded. "I get being under a lot of stress because of cheer stuff. But you really think people don't expect you to have other things you like doing?"

"I didn't just stop because I was worried about what the squad would think. I stopped because . . ." she took a breath. "when I do something, it pretty much has to be all or nothing."

"Yeah, I've noticed," I said, thinking about the way

GIVE ME AN 83!

she went after me so hardcore when she found out Bevan and I had been out on a couple of dates. And whenever I look at her at practice, she is crazy intense. Like nothing can take her focus off the mat.

"So I'm making a choice," Katie continued. "I'm going back to dance. And the school I'm auditioning to get into has one of the best modern dance programs in the world. But seriously," she said, her voice dropping to a whisper, as if someone were trying to listen in, "if the Titans find out about this, they'll bug out. I mean, I'll tell them if I get in, but for now, can we keep this between us?"

This was waaaay too much scoop for me to swallow in just one bite.

Mrs. Parker shouted across the lobby, interrupting us. "Katherine Anne Parker, if we don't leave now, they won't let you in. No late arrivals!"

Katie made an annoyed face. "We're not late!" she shouted back. Then, turning to me, she said, "Listen, I gotta go. But please, please don't tell anyone I'm here, or anything that I told you, ok?"

She ran out, leaving me in the lobby feeling completely stunned.

First of all, this is **HUGE.** Katie not wanting to be a Titan anymore? And second of all, her having this,

GIVE ME AN 84!

like, secret dance thing going on all this time? Whoa. And the biggest kicker: she wants **ME** to keep her little secret for her. What am I, her new bestie?

Must be the New York air or something, but for some reason I'm actually not dying to get on the phone and spread the word—even though this is one extra-juicy piece of gossip. A part of me feels bad for Katie— it must be hard

for her to have to choose between cheer and dance. (I know I feel that way sometimes when it comes to cheer and fashion design.) Katie loves that squad so much. And cheer has been, like, her entire life—or so I thought.

Finally, Dad and Beth came downstairs in their usual lovey-dovey hand-holding way.

"What took so long?" I complained, even though I was kind of glad they'd taken so long. Otherwise I wouldn't have found out Katie's big secret.

"Sorry," said Beth. "I got a call from work."

"Hey, Mads, are you ok?" asked Dad.

I am super readable when it comes to my emotions.

"Oh, yeah. Just ran into someone from school." I

GIVE ME AN 85!

shrugged. I knew Dad could tell there was something more, but luckily, he didn't push it. Besides, I was still kind of processing everything and didn't feel like telling them. I don't think they'd understand what the big deal is anyway.

Well, we're almost at our stop. Going to this downtown neighborhood called SoHo! Bevan said there's supposed to be a lot of cute stores there . . . and we all know how much I heart shopping!

LUNCH, BALTHAZAR RESTAURANT

When we got out of the subway, there was a whole band of guys playing drums right on the subway platform. They were perched on some overturned crates, just banging away, hair swaying back and forth, totally getting lost in their music. While Dad and Beth went to the newsstand to get bottled waters, one guy, who was holding a bunch of the band's CDs, came right up to me.

"This. Is. Reggae," he said, shoving a CD in my hand.

I just smiled back at him stupidly, not knowing what to say.

"Now <u>you</u> are someone who digs the reggae, ja mon?" he said with a smile.

I was just about to say thank you and walk away

GIVE ME AN
86!

with the CD when the guy stopped me. "Miss, miss," he said, grabbing the CD back from my hand. "Usually we receive donations for these." All traces of his Rasta accent were suddenly gone.

"Donations?" I asked dumbly.

Before he could answer, another guy came up to us, clutching a Sharpie in his hand, and said, "What's your name? Who should I make this out to?"

"Um, Madison?" I said nervously.

What was taking Dad so long???

"To Mad Madison," said the guy with a chuckle as he wrote out my name on the CD.

Then the first guy was like, "We usually get about fifteen bucks for our CDs. Do you have something like that on you?"

"Um, no," I stammered. "Sorry." T.G. I saw Dad coming back. "I gotta go!" I said, and booked it over to Dad and Beth.

"Everything all right?" asked Beth, looking concerned.

How embarrassing! They left me alone for two minutes and I'd gotten myself into a sitch.

"Yeah," I said, eager to get out of the subway and into fresh air. "I made the mistake of thinking those guys were giving away their CDs for free. And I don't

GIVE ME AN 87!

even like reggae. I was just being nice!"

Beth laughed, and Dad shook his head. "Rookie mistake," said Dad. "New York Rule Number One: Don't take anything from strangers on the street. Nothing is free."

"Thanks for letting me know in advance," I quipped.

We went inside the most adorbs French bakery for walnut bread and croissants—but again, I was stuck standing superclose to the person in line in front of me. Maybe New Yorkers have a special need to be in extremely close physical contact with each other? Must have something to do with what they say about city life being lonely.

But seriously, Soho was so cool. I can't believe that I ever thought of myself as "in the know," when it came to trends and stuff. This part of New York went **WAY** beyond my wildest dreams with all its amazing clothes. All the styles I had been salivating over from magazines and street style blogs were right there in the windows of nearly every boutique on the side streets we walked down. I went inside one store where everything was handmade by the designer who owns it. I was like, "Can I have your life?" I bought a pair of uh-mazing over-the-knee boots in suede in one of the last stores we went into. Sigh.

GIVE ME AN 88!

I was so inspired by the amazing shoes, skirts, jewelry, and cute hats that when we finally sat down to lunch I just couldn't stop sketching in my journal. I wanted to capture it all before I could forget. So far, I've sketched all my favorite styles from the day so that I'll be able to look them up when I go back to Port Angeles and try to recreate them at home. (Oh, because as FABULOUS as all the clothes here are, they are mucho dinero.) As I was sketching, I realized that I haven't actually sewn anything in forever. I can't even remember the last time I sat down at my sewing machine. There must be dust piled up to three feet on top of that thing.

I could hear Katie's voice in my head as I sketched away: "Dance is my passion. But I haven't been able to keep up with it." I think the reason that Katie being here is so shocking to me is that I just can't imagine

GIVE ME AN 89!

someone like her, who is at the top of her game, wanting to do something **ELSE** more than cheer. For me at least, cheer has become, like, the most important thing **EVER**. I've always loved creating my own clothes, but I've let that passion die down since I've been so busy with the Grizzlies. I guess there's no way you can do both at 100%. In a way, I'm kind of like Katie. If I'm going to do something, I have to give it my all—so that's probably why I've let the design stuff sit on the back burner. I wonder what would happen if I decided to go back to fashion design? Could I ever leave cheer if I had the chance to do fashion stuff seriously?

I was mid-sketch when Dad said, "Hon, I know you're busy drawing, but can Beth and I interrupt you for a minute?"

(PS—I get annoyed when Dad calls what I

GIVE ME A 90!

do "drawing." Like I'm some five-year-old with crayons, doodling on a place mat.)

"Yeah. Sure," I said, closing my journal.

Dad took a deep breath and looked over at Beth. She put her hand over his, and then they gave each other these big, gooey smiles. "So," said Dad. "Beth and I have some news to share with you."

"Oh God, oh God, oh God. Please no!" I thought. "Please do not be engaged!!!"

I was completely bulldozed over the last time he said he wanted to talk to me—but luckily, that time he just wanted to invite me on this trip. Suddenly, it was all making sense. He must have invited me so he could tell me that he and Beth were tying the ol' knot. My worst nightmare coming true. I was seriously about to barf up my yummy sandwich right there, all over my sketchbook. And, if I do say so myself, those sketches were pretty sweet. I could just see Dad being like, "And the best part is: You're going to be the flower girl!" Ha-ha. That would be hysterical. I'd do a little cheer down the aisle, complete with backflips, as I threw the flower petals around. Just perrrfect.

"We are moving to New York City!" he announced proudly. Then he looked at Beth and back at me. "That's why we brought you here on this vacation, actually."

GIVE ME A
911!

Ohhhhhh. Huh?

I wanted to be like, "Excuse me? Need a little more info here, please. And what does this have to do with me? Way to keep me in the loop before you made this ginormous decision." But all I said was, "Wha-huh?"

"Your father got an amazing job offer here," Beth said, beaming. Her eyes sparkled with excitement. In fact, I've never seen Business Beth so filled with joy. "I've asked to be transferred to our sister company here. They're paying for the move and everything!" she exclaimed.

Dad looked at Beth again, and then at me. "And we wanted you to see what it was like here. In case, you know . . ." He looked down at his lap almost shyly, like he was afraid how I would react. "In case you wanted to come here too," he continued.

Talk about being bulldozed. I was flat as a pancake. "As in, move here with you? To New York?"

Dad nodded. "Yes, we'd love you to just consider

GIVE ME A 92!

it. Beth and I even picked up some brochures for you about schools that specialize in the arts. But no pressure. It's just an option you have now."

I looked around at all the amazingly cool-looking people sitting in the maroon-colored banquettes all along the walls, clinking glasses with each other, and eating oysters from towers that were five feet tall. All this could be MY life?

I could tell that Dad and Beth were waiting for me to respond. But out of nowhere, a horrible, horrible feeling rushed over me. I was suddenly furious at Dad for springing this on me. How long had he been waiting to tell me something this important? And he had to take me on vacation to do it?

The words poured out of my mouth before I could stop them. "You already left Mom and me once. Now you want to run away again? All the way to New York? And you're telling me it's an 'option' for me to come too? C'mon, Dad! You know Mom would never go for it. My whole life is in Port Angeles. Maybe you can pick up and leave behind things that are important to you. But me? I can't do that."

I regretted the words as soon as I said them. Wasn't I the one just fantasizing about bringing fashion design back into my life? And now that I was being

GIVE ME A 93!

given the opportunity, I was freaking out about it.

I noticed that the people from the next table over were looking at us.

Dad looked totally deflated. "Honey, I'm not leaving you," he said, putting his hand on my shoulder. "This is a good step for my career. And Beth and I truly would love for you to live with us. But I understand if it's too much to take in at once."

"Sorry. I didn't mean to . . . I just . . . need to think about all this. Can you excuse me?" I said, getting up from the table, and trying not to knock over the glasses on the table next to ours as I slid past them. I needed a little break, so I went downstairs to the bathroom to pull myself back together.

As I neared the ladies' room, my phone vibrated in my pocket.

It was a text from Bevan (which kind of annoyed me, because secretly I was hoping it was E). "Heeeeyyy u. Haven't heard from u in a while. How's city life? Did u pierce your nose + start going to poetry readings yet?"

"Heyyyy!" I texted back. "NYC is awesome. I heart it. But my dad and Beth are driving me crazy!"

"☹."

"I'll tell u all abt it ltr. V-chat 2nite?"

GIVE ME A
94!

"Yeppers. Later skater."

By the time I was done chatting with Bevan, I felt slightly better. But Bevan doesn't really get everything that's gone down in my family—not like Evan does. He would totally understand why I'm so upset with my dad. (Probably even better than I understand it myself.) Well, at least the ladies' room had some nice rose-scented hand lotion and After Eight mints. Free stuff always makes me happy.

AFTERNOON, MUSEUM GIFT SHOP

After **THE FIGHT**, we went to an awesome little museum that was actually in an old mansion on Fifth Avenue. I know that Beth and Dad were bothered by how quiet I'd been since lunch, and probably wanted to talk about what I'd said earlier. But lucky moi, I didn't have to explain myself because we each had these great little walkie-talkies that we listened to on our tour of the museum. It was so cool—you just pressed a button corresponding to the number on the painting, and the whole history of the painting came pouring into your ear! Can someone **PLEASE** start making these things for boys, too? Wouldn't it be cool if you could point a walkie-talkie at your best guy friend and press a button to find out why he's been acting so weird

GIVE ME A 95!

lately? (But seriously, why has he not written to me AT ALL???)

My absolute favorite part of the museum was this one room called the Fragonard Room, which was a re-created version of a lady's parlor from waaaaaay back when. All the furniture looked like it was covered in gold, from the edges of the chairs to the legs of the tables. And all over the walls there were these beautiful paintings by this Fragonard guy, which basically showed a man and a woman flirting with each other. The whole room was colored in pastels. According to my super-duper walkie-talkie, the style of the room and the art was called "rococo." Which to me, is basically as super girly as it gets in terms of style. I think Lanie would freak out if she saw this room—it is the EXACT OPPOSITE of the kind of room she would ever want to live in. Not a goth object in sight here! (Except now that her room has turned into a teenybopper-inspired Dustin Barker shrine, maybe she would like this after all!) What I do know? I would have totally A-DORED living in that room if I had been alive during that time period. Except for the giant dresses that everyone wore back then. Just imagine cheering in one of those things!

GIVE ME A 96!

NIGHTTIME, HOTEL LOBBY

Whoa. Intense meeting with my Grizzly clan this afternoon. I signed onto chat just in time—I had to practically sprint upstairs to my room because it took us **FOREVER** to get back from the museum. When I signed on, the entire team was already there waiting for me in front of the little window of my chat screen. As soon as the video came on, Matt and Ian made stupid faces at me and yelled, "Hiiii, Madison." But Jared and Tabitha Sue looked worried. Katarina looked downright nervous. I guess they didn't take the news of our "emergency meeting" lightly.

Before we got down to business, I gave them the "grand tour" of my room and showed them the view from my window (I didn't even have to move the computer—I just tilted the screen. Ha-ha!). Gotta impress the team with my digs.

"It looks so New York-y over there!" said Tabitha Sue.

"Well, that's cuz it is." I smiled. "Look, over there is Central Park. Can you see it?" I pointed my computer to the corner of the window that would give them the best view.

When I turned the computer back around, Ian's face took up the screen. He was shaking his head. "Didn't see anything."

GIVE ME A
97!

"Hmm," I said. "Probably hard to see over the computer."

"Take pictures!" said Jared, from the back of the crowd.

"All right, everyone," said Jacqui, pushing Ian out of the frame. "Madison and I have something to tell you, and we didn't want to do this without Maddy being here, so . . ."

"I know, I know," said Matt. "You're both in love with me and don't know how to decide who gets me. It's all right, there's enough of me for each of you," he said smugly.

"Thanks for that, Matt," I said. "But that won't be necessary. This problem has to do with the squad."

"Awww, but Madison, you're on vacation!" said Tabitha Sue sweetly. "You should be enjoying yourself. Not worrying about us Grizzlies. I'm sure Jacqui could have done the meeting without you."

"Thanks, Tabitha Sue. But as your co-captain, it's important for me to be present. At least in some way."

She nodded.

"And trust me, I'm having cheer withdrawal for sure," I assured her. "I like thinking about cheer stuff while I'm here. It's totally no prob."

Katarina already knew that she was the subject

GIVE ME A
98!

of the meeting. It would have been über awkward (and mean!) to just bring that up in front of the whole team (kind of like how Dad dumped his little news on me at lunch). But she hadn't told anyone yet—not even Tabitha Sue. Big virtual high five to good ol' Katarina.

VIRTUAL HIGH FIVE!

"Here's the deal," said Jacqui. "You know how each squad member has to get at least a B- in each class in order for the team to qualify for the Get Up and Cheer competition?"

There was a chorus of "yeahs" and "uh-huhs" from the different squad members.

"Well, unfortunately, one of us didn't make that cut."

Everyone looked at one another suspiciously.

Katarina looked down at her toes. Then she lifted her head and spoke up. "It vas me," she said softly. "I didn't

GIVE ME A 99!

gain ze good grades." She covered her face with her hands.

Jacqui patted Katarina on the back. "Hey, don't worry about it. It'll all work out."

I explained to the team that not only were we in danger of being cut from the competition, but Katarina might have to leave the squad if her grades didn't improve.

"Nice going, Katarina," said Matt. "Way to learn the English language."

"Yeah, thanks, Katarina," said Jared. "I've been looking forward to this forever! This was going to be my big debut!" He looked out into the distance, as if he were seeing some imaginary audience applauding.

"Don't be so selfish," Jacqui said, looking at Jared and Matt. "Both of you, apologize. We don't talk that way to our teammates."

"Yes, Mom," said Matt, rolling his eyes. "Sorry, Katarina."

"Yeah, sorry," said Jared, just as insincerely.

"You are ok," said Katarina gloomily.

I knew I needed to get the team's collective mind off the blame game and into "can do" mode. STAT.

"All right guys, here's the plan," I said. "We're going to help Katarina study for the big test coming up so

GIVE ME A 100!

that she can ace it and raise her grade. If we get her grade up before the competition, we're safe. We have to work together, though."

"Hey, I didn't sign up to be anyone's tutor," said Ian defensively.

"You didn't sign up for cheerleading, period," barked Jacqui. "You don't have a choice, remember? Your football coach made you a Grizzly. Now act like someone who's actually part of a team."

Ian blushed with embarrassment. Both he and Matt hate when we bring up the whole getting-kicked-off-the-football-team thing. But Jacqui and I know it's always a good way to get them to be respectful.

"We're going to make sure you rock that next test," Jacqui told Katarina confidently.

Tabitha Sue smiled encouragingly. "I'm in," she said, raising her hand like she was in class.

"Good," I said, relieved. "We were hoping you could share some of your social studies geniusness with Katarina."

Katarina smiled at Tabitha Sue.

"And you," said Jacqui, pointing to Matt. "You're going to help her memorize facts. We know that's a secret skill of yours." She winked.

Matt sighed, but nodded "ok."

GIVE ME A
101!

"And we'll all take turns teaching Katarina the chapters on the test," I said.

"It will help you guys study too," said Jacqui. "So it's a win-win!"

I could tell Jacqui was trying to be Miss Positive. It worked—mostly.

Jared pushed his way in front of the team so his face took up my entire screen. "No offense, Katarina," he said, looking over his shoulder at her, then back to the screen. "I love you, but me being a drama king and all . . . well, like I said, I'm dying to get into this competition and show off how amazing I've gotten at cheer. Right now everyone thinks we're a joke. But we're not—and this competition is our one chance to prove it. But if this 'plan' doesn't work out, and you don't pass your test, I think we need to have a backup person. Just in case."

I hadn't even considered that option—and I know Jacqui hadn't either. I think we come from the same "stand by your teammate" school of thought. In my mind, either Katarina would pass and we'd all go to the competition together, or she wouldn't, and we'd have to wait for another one—maybe one with different regulations. But it looked like Jared went to a different school of thought: The Jared Handler Is the Most

GIVE ME A 102!

Important Person in the World School.

"What do you mean, backup person?" asked Tabitha Sue warily.

Jared nodded patiently. "Like an understudy. Who we bring in and train, and if Katarina doesn't pass, then we still get to go to this competition."

I know that as a captain, I have to be open-minded to each squad member's ideas. I didn't want to come across as just favoring Katarina. Even though I'm not thrilled with the idea, Jared definitely had a good point. If there is a way we can still go to the Get Up and Cheer! competition, then we need to consider it.

"It's not a bad idea," I said slowly. "But our first priority should be to our teammate. And everyone needs to pitch in."

"Don't worry," said Tabitha Sue, patting Katarina on the shoulder. "I won't let you fail. Trust me, with my help we won't need an 'understudy,'" she said, making quote marks in the air.

"Katarina, are you ok with this plan?" Jacqui asked. Katarina shrugged.

"Paging Captain Not-So-Obvious," said Ian. "Exactly who are we going to find as a backup cheerleader over winter break? The whole school is on vacation, and whoever isn't on vacation is on some sports team."

GIVE ME A 103!

"Ahem," said Jared, puffing out his chest proudly. "Jared to the rescue, again. I already have someone in mind from drama class. And they're around practicing for the school play. She's actually been a gymnast her whole life, and has some great dance moves."

"If they're anything like yours, then we're in trouble," quipped Matt.

"Ha-ha," said Jared sarcastically.

We decided to have another meeting tomorrow to meet Jared's friend and have her try out for the team.

"Then we'll all take a vote," said Jacqui.

Everyone agreed. I could tell Tabitha Sue was the least on board about this alternate cheerleader idea. Even less so than Katarina. Tabitha Sue is a loyal friend and teammate to the core. I heart her.

Before signing off, Jacqui told the rest of the team to start stretching without her. She got up real close to the speaker so she could whisper. "So, any developments with that thing we were talking about before?" she said with a wink, referring to the Katie sighting.

I really wasn't feeling so good about lying to my friend and co-captain, but I felt like I should keep Katie's business a secret. At least for now. I could

GIVE ME A 104!

always tell Jacqui when I got home.

"Nope!" I said, with probably a little too much enthusiasm. "Haven't seen her since that last time. Must have been my imagination. I doubt it's her."

Even though I'm one terrible liar, Jacqui actually seemed to believe me. Probs because the whole sitch is completely **INSANE** and totally unlikely to **EVER** occur in real life.

"Oh, too bad," she said. "I wouldn't have minded hearing some dirt about my old captain."

As soon as I signed off, Mom called me. She isn't attending every winter break practice, so I filled her in on Jared's big idea.

"Oh, don't worry about Jared," said Mom. "I spoke to Mrs. Tuttle today, and she says if Katarina scores a B+ or more on that next test, and comes to extra helps over break, she'll drop her worst grade."

"That's amazing, Mom! You're awesome!" My mom really is the bomb diggity sometimes.

"I think it's great how you guys are all coming together to help your teammate out," said Mom.

"Of course," I said. "She's our girl. Too bad Jared doesn't feel the same way."

"Well, you know Jared," said Mom. "He still has a lot to learn about teamwork. It'll come to him at some point.

GIVE ME A 105!

At least the rest of the team is supportive." Mom is always Mrs. Bright Side.

"I didn't like his idea, but I felt bad just saying no to it, you know?"

"I understand," she said. "You'll figure out the right thing to do."

I hope so.

I wasn't in the mood to tell her about the life-changing announcement Dad had made earlier today. I'm pretty sure that he hasn't mentioned his plans to her—otherwise she DEF would have said something to me. She knows I don't like surprises. Especially when it comes to Dad. It's just, I know she'll completely lose it if she thinks I'm considering moving away from her (not that I am, because I'm totally not . . . right?). She'll think I'm, like, choosing him over her, and I SOOOOO can't deal with that right now. Not to mention the fact that the second she finds out, she'll call him and completely decimate him for not discussing something as crazy important as this with her first. Therefore, I've decided there's no need to freak her out while I'm here. After we caught up, I told her I had to get ready for dinner. Which I did, so it wasn't exactly a lie.

GIVE ME A
106!

On the way to the restaurant I called Lanie.

"Sup, chica?" asked Lanes.

"Let me just say it has been quite a day."

"What's going on?" she asked, with concern in her voice.

"Well, first of all, I spoke to Katie this morning."

"So I guess the whole hiding-in-your-room-all-week thing didn't quite work out?" said Lanie.

"No, not so much." I told Lanie about my convo with Katie and how she totally lied about visiting her grandparents. "Turns out Katie has a secret dance passion. She's auditioning to go to school here."

"Shut up!" cried Lanie. "Seriously?"

"Seriously."

"Wow. That is pretty out there. Huh, who knew you'd go to New York and get a backstage pass to 'The Secret Life of Katie Parker,'" Lanie mused.

"Apparently her being here is a ginormous secret from the Titans. We can't tell anyone, got it?"

"Who am I going to tell? All my cheerleader friends?" Lanie asked sarcastically.

"Just don't write about it in the Daily Angeles," I joked. "I'm sworn to secrecy.

"Secret's safe," said Lanie. "Besides, even if I wanted to dish this, you have way too much on me.

GIVE ME A
107!

Imagine what this whole secret romance with Dustin Barker would do to my rep at school?"

"I wouldn't exactly call it a romance, since he doesn't know it's happening."

"Details, details."

"Hey, Lanes. Have you heard anything from E?"

"You mean, have I spoken to him? Yeah. He's bored out of his mind." She chuckled. "Like most of us who aren't on snazzy New York vacations."

"Oh, that's nice," I said glumly. "He's _so_ busy being bored out of his mind he can't even e-mail me?"

"What do you mean?" asked Lanie.

I remembered then that I haven't told Lanie about the awkward night at E's house, or how he seemed to be avoiding me since. I could have told her right then, but I decided I don't want to put her in the middle of the two of us again. It didn't work out too well that time when E had me starring as an evil villain fighting against the fabulous Katie Parker SuperGirl in an installment of his SuperBoy comic and I begged Lanes to dish all the dirt on why. Lanie **HATES** being in the middle (who can blame her??). Besides, he obviously didn't tell her anything either.

"Oh, never mind," I said. "So, dare I ask . . . how was the book signing?"

GIVE ME A 108!

"Ohmigod, he is even cuuuuuter in person!" Lanie gushed.

"Oh, boo. I was hoping you'd discover he didn't actually write his book and get over him," I sighed.

"Seriously, Mads," she squealed. "I almost couldn't talk when I brought my book over for him to sign!"

"Might that be because you waited on line for eight hours before you got up to him, and were parched?"

Lanie laughed. "Um. Yeah. That might have had something to do with it."

"So? What happened?" I asked. We were almost at the restaurant, so I had to speed the convo up.

"Get this. He wrote, 'Dear Lanie Marks. You are a sweet girl. Stay cute!'"

"Awww. True love."

"I know!"

"I was joking!" I said. But it was no use. This Dustin Barker thing had gotten into all the sane circuits of her brain and rewired them. "Ok, now that you've seen him and gotten his autograph, you realize that the two of you are just not going to happen, right?"

"No!" she protested. "I'm more in luuurve than ever."

GIVE ME A 109!

"Lanie, the boy wears pink shirts. You <u>hate</u> pink."

"I'm making an exception."

I made a note that as soon as I got back to Port Angeles, we'd have to cruise some poetry readings or something more Lanie-ish for cute boys so she could move on from this Dustin thing.

GIVE ME A
110!

Thursday, January 5

Afternoon, (the heartbreak hotel) room

Holiday Cheer!

Give me an S-N-O-W!

When I woke up, it was actually **SNOWING** outside. Right outside my window, there were these huuuuge, fat flakes falling on all the buildings. How magical! Just like Bevan said it would be.

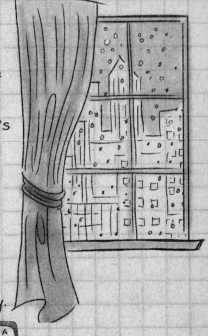

Just then the phone rang, and I almost just picked up the phone and said, "Dad, give me, like, five minutes!" (Because he's an early birdie and likes to hit the pavement when it's still dark out.) But it wasn't Dad.

"Hey, it's Katie," said the very un-Dad-like voice on the phone.

"Uh . . . ," was all I could say.

GIVE ME A
IIII!

Katie Parker? Calling **ME**? Insanity.

"I was just was wondering if . . . maybe you'd want to chill for a bit?"

"Uh, with me?" I asked stupidly.

And this, folks, is what happens when I try to talk to popular cheerleaders before I've eaten my breakfast. Actually, let's be honest—this probably would have happened to me even on a full stomach of sustenance. Why, oh why, am I so low IQ sometimes?

"Uh, yes. You," she said.

I didn't have any plans for breakfast, so I said yes. (Also, I was a little intrigued . . . Katie Parker wanted to hang out with **ME**. Weird.) I told Dad I was meeting up with a school friend who happened to be in the hotel, and he was super happy.

"Oh, how nice!" he exclaimed to Beth over the phone (rather loudly). "Maddy has a friend in this very hotel!"

Yeah. That's code for, "Did you hear that, Beth darling, my daughter actually isn't a giant loser with no friends like we'd originally thought." Awesome. Ok, maybe my interpretation of him is a slight exaggeration, but there's definitely some truth to it.

Anyway, Dad and I decided to meet in an hour or so, so I went downstairs, grabbed a bagel, and met Katie in the hotel library (the only place where there's some

GIVE ME A
112!

actual privacy in this teensy hotel). When I got there, Katie was sprawled out on a love seat like she owned the place. She was dressed in another dance outfit: This time she had a ripped oversize T-shirt over a tank top, and baggy sweatpants.

"Oh, hey," she said, barely looking up from the magazine on her lap when I walked in. Like SHE was surprised that I was there, as if I had followed her in there like one of her adoring fans. I wanted to be like, "Um, you were the one who asked to hang with me. Not the other way around."

But all I said was, "Hey."

"It is so boring here," she said, throwing her head back dramatically. "There's, like, nothing to do."

I walked over to the bookshelves to see if there was anything interesting to read. Even though I was pretty sure there wouldn't be any books about cheerleading or fashion design ☹.

"Really? I don't feel like that at all," I said. "We've been doing tons of stuff, but I'm sure we've, like, barely scratched the surface of amazing things to do in New York. I can't imagine being bored here."

"Oh, like, touristy stuff," said Katie, all snottily. "I'm so over that. I've been here, like, a million times." She picked up her magazine again.

GIVE ME A 113!

"Well, I haven't." I shrugged. Nice. So Katie basically invited me down here so she could boast about what a real New Yorker she is.

"So, how'd the audition go?" I asked, trying to change the subject.

I could see Katie's expression change from totally under control to kind of unsteady. Guess I found her weakness.

"Actually, my first audition is later today," she said, suddenly chewing on a nail. "I'm kind of nervous. The auditions this week will pretty much make or break me getting into the Dance and Music Academy."

"What do you mean?" I asked.

Katie placed her chin on her hands. "It's crazy. Basically, I have two chances to impress the school. The first audition is ballet. And the second is modern. I'm really nervous for ballet, though. I'm not that into it. It's just never been my thing, and I'm worried the judges will be able to tell."

"Oh, come on!" I replied. "You're, like, a ridiculously amazing dancer. I'm sure you're going to blow those judges' minds. I mean, now that I think about it, haven't you brought some ballet moves into your Titan routines? That's pretty awesome."

Katie smiled. "Thanks. It's really nice of you to say

GIVE ME A 114!

all that. I guess I'm good at ballet. But since it's not my fave type of dance, it makes me nervous. It just doesn't feel as natural."

"I get it. But honestly, I'm pretty sure you're going to be awesome at whatever dance you do." I wasn't just trying to be nice, either. Katie is an amazing dancer, and it shows through her cheerleading. Whenever I get a chance to glimpse the Titans practicing, I'm always **TOTALLY** blown away by how graceful she is. It's like she's completely weightless or something. It's weird that after all the time I've spent watching her, I never wondered where all that dance ability came from.

Katie threw up her hands. "Thanks, Madison. I just wish I wasn't so freaked out. And my mom is, like, no help at all. She makes me even more nervous—which is almost impossible at this point. I've literally never been this nervous in my life. Not even for Nationals! Maybe it's because in cheer, you have a whole team to rely on, you know? You're not alone. And if something goes wrong, it's not all on one person. But here? It's like, they're judging me and me alone. If I don't get it, there's only one reason."

"Ah . . . I see. So that's why you invited me down here," I joked. "Because you have no one else to talk to!" (Um, I can't believe I actually had the nerve to say that

GIVE ME A
115!

out loud! Sure I was joking, but normally I would never have the guts to be like that! Guess being on vacation lets you let go a little.)

"No, it's not like that at all." She buried her head in her hands. "I figured you'd understand, since you're a cheerleader too. You know what it's like to psych yourself out of something."

SO . . . I know it's kind of dorky of me (not that that's surprising), but the fact that she actually acknowledged me as a fellow cheerleader made me feel pretty good. Also, it was good to know she wasn't just using me as a sounding board because I'm not her mom. She actually seems to care about what I think.

"Listen, whenever I've doubted my ability is when I've messed up an audition. I mean, you saw me at cheer tryouts. I was so nervous, I ended up messing up big-time."

Katie laughed.

"So, you just have to go in there knowing that you're going to own it. You have the skills. You just need to believe in them. You're going to be awesome."

"You're just being nice," said Katie.

"Um, not really," I said. "I've watched you more times than I'd like to admit at practice. You just have that extra something that the other girls don't. I know you're going to ace these auditions. You just have to

GIVE ME A 116!

stop psyching yourself out."

Katie shook her head. "No one's ever said anything like that to me. Not even my best friends."

I just shrugged. I mean, it doesn't surprise me. Her best friends are Clementine and Hilary—of course they'd never say anything like that. Still, I couldn't exactly bash them at that moment. I didn't really know what else to say. "Just being honest," I said.

We looked through some magazines Katie had brought with her, and tried to find something to read that didn't say "Economics Today" or "World News" on it. Before I knew it, Dad came by looking for me.

"You ready?" he asked. Then he registered Katie, "You must be Madison's friend. Hi, I'm Mr. Hays."

Katie introduced herself to Dad. Awkward! Wouldn't it be awesome if parents could just go about their lives without ever having to talk to our friends?

"Good luck today," I told Katie as I left. "Let me know how it goes."

"Totally," she said.

After my unexpected morning, I went with Beth and Dad to ogle the Macy's windows. It turns out that Beth is obsessed with them. "I've gone to see them every year since I was a little girl. It used to be this tradition I had with my dad," she said.

GIVE ME A
117!

The windows didn't look that magical to me—they just looked like a good excuse to advertise fancy designer brands. I'm not big into labels, I guess. I'd much rather find something that no one else has. Or make it myself.

But we had to go into the store anyway because Beth wanted perfume and a new handbag. Normally I would never say no to a shopping spree, but the crowds there made it less than fun. Another sardine experience for Maddy! I'd much rather go back to Soho and shop in the smaller boutiques. They have stuff that I could never find at home. But I will say that Beth chose a cool bag. Maybe she has pretty decent taste after all.

After we left Macy's, we passed a Barnes & Noble and I saw an ad for this new graphic novel that Evan was talking about nonstop a couple weeks ago. Actually, I haven't asked Evan how SuperBoy is going in a long time, now that I think about it. Is he working on a new one? Is he still even interested in making more SuperBoys? How do I **NOT** know these things? Sure, he has been pretty bad about being in touch with me, but I guess I haven't been the best of friends either. In his mind it must look like I lost interest once the funds from SuperBoy stopped benefiting the Grizzlies' uniforms anymore. Ugh. That's just great. I'm so glad my best

GIVE ME A 118!

friend thinks I used him for his talents and then threw him away. I **MUST** talk to him about this when I get back.

"Do you guys mind if I go in for a sec?" I asked Beth and Dad.

In the meantime, perhaps a little "I'm sorry" gift will help our friendship. Maybe it will show him that he's still a big part of my life and that I'm thinking about him. Grrr. Why is everything so complicated?

As soon as I handed over my moola to the cashier, I texted Evan.

"So guess who's the proud owner of a much-aniticipated new graphic novel?"

"Ur kidding. They're not on sale yet at the Book Worm."

I was so relieved that he wrote back right away. A part of me was worried he would take, like, a day to respond.

"Aaaannnd it's signed!"

"Whoa. Thanks Maddy ☺!" he wrote back. "Heyyyy. U havin' fun?"

"Yah," I wrote. I didn't want him to know that I was upset that he hadn't contacted me at all since I got here. Or that it was kind of affecting my good time. "Havin' a blast."

"Cool," he wrote back.

GIVE ME A 119!

But now? I'm, like, checking my phone every two minutes to see if he'll write anything more but so far, **NOTHING. ZIP. NADA.** Complete cell phone silence. Seriously. **WHY DO I CARE SO MUCH?**

Anyway, more later. Right now I gotta jet back to the hotel. Virtual Grizzly meeting awaits!

LATER, HOTEL LOBBY

T.G. I made sure we had enough time to get back before my Grizzly meeting. This public transportation situation is not a good way to get somewhere on time. I have to hand it to Dad and Beth—it's like anything I ask for they say yes to. Maybe they're trying to sweet-talk me into coming to New York for good. Ever since my little outburst yesterday at the restaurant, Dad has been super-duper nice to me.

The big thing on my mind as soon as we started the meeting was how things were going with Katarina and the tutoring.

"Yo, yo, yo!" shouted Jacqui as soon as the video came on. I couldn't see her, though, just Jared

GIVE ME A 120!

absentmindedly scratching his butt because he didn't know he was facing the screen.

"Move closer, I can't see you!" I said.

Jacqui put her face all the way up to the video monitor so I could practically see up her nose. "Better?" she joked.

"Oh, yeah. Oodles. Ok, so, Katarina, how's the tutoring going?" Jacqui moved away so I could see Katarina better.

Katarina looked way better than she had the day before. Yesterday she seemed pretty depressed. Today she had back her usual confidence. She held her shoulders back proudly. "Oh, yes. I am having good tutoring."

"She's doing great," said Tabitha Sue, smiling at Katarina. "I think she gets nervous when Mrs. T. explains it. Because of the language thing. But she's comfortable with her friends, so it's different when we go over the material."

"Tabitha Sue is good teacher." Katarina beamed.

"Well, Matt, you're up tonight."

Matt nodded in agreement. "If I have to . . ."

"We don't have much time," Jacqui pointed out. "The test is the first day back from break."

"Hey, guys, she's here," interrupted Jared. He waved

GIVE ME A 12!!

at someone I couldn't see offscreen, and then pulled her over to the computer. "Everyone, this is Diane Huerta."

Diane has beautiful long black hair and big brown eyes. And definitely a gymnast's physique.

"Oh, hey," I said. "I know you. We had math together last year." Our school is so big that you might not know someone in your grade unless you have a class with them. Kind of crazy.

"Oh. Right! I remember," said Diane. She addressed me and the rest of the team. "Well, I'm Diane. A friend of Jared's. I have some dance and gymnastics background—but I haven't really done any of that in a while," she said apologetically.

"Hey, don't sweat it," said Jacqui.

Diane shrugged and smiled. "So, Jared told me I should prepare something for a tryout today. I didn't have much time, but here goes."

Everyone cleared away so that I'd have a good view.

Diane started her routine with a series of backflips, and then some pretty awesome toe touch fulls. The expression on her face the whole time was like a little kid who'd just opened the best Christmas present ever. It was total Cheer Face, the way you're **SUPPOSED** to look when you're cheering (and which the Grizzlies

GIVE ME A
122!

kind of slack off on a lot of the time). Then she did a little cheer that she borrowed from the Titans, with some cute dance moves and hand motions:

WE'RE THE TITANS.

WE'RE RED, WHITE, AND BLUE.

WE'RE GOING TO ROCK THE HOUSE TONIGHT.

HOW ABOUT YOU?

She ended the routine with a couple more tumbles, and pointed to the audience (well, me) when she said the "you" in "how about you?"

It looked like she'd been practicing the routine for months. For someone who hasn't done gymnastics in a long time, she's a natural. Each movement was well timed and airtight. As soon as she finished, the whole team started clapping exuberantly—especially Katarina. I even heard some clapping from the other side of the gym— guess the Titans had been watching too.

Diane blushed and took a bow.

"Whoa! Nice job!" I said into the camera. Even though we knew she was going to prepare something, Jacqui and I assumed we'd have to ask her to do some other stunts and cheers, just to be sure. But it looked like we were wrong. . . .

She's clearly capable—and will definitely be an asset to our team.

GIVE ME A 123!

"Wow! Vere deed you learn ze gymnastics?" asked Katarina, who seemed psyched to have found someone else with her background.

"I used to take gymnastics in my old town, in Colorado. I was a gymnastics freak then. . . . But when I moved here I found the whole drama scene." She smiled at Jared. "Obviously."

She told the team that she's always wanted to get into cheerleading because it seems like a perfect way to combine her passion for performing on stage and her love of gymnastics. "Because, you know, there's lots of drama in cheer, too," she joked. "I was going to try out last year, but the whole Titan clique really got on my nerves. And besides, they would never give a theater geek like me a chance," she said, matter-of-factly.

"Well, that's what the Grizzlies are for," said Tabitha Sue. "We're the band of misfits."

"Hey, now," said Jacqui.

"I was just kidding," said Tabitha Sue, her face turning pink.

We asked Diane if she wouldn't mind stepping outside while the team voted. She'd barely shut the door to the gym before the whole team raised their hands in a vote of YES.

GIVE ME A 124!

"Ok," I said. "So it looks like Diane is a no-brainer. She's on the team, if she'll have us."

Everyone nodded.

"Jared, wanna go grab her?" I asked. Jared sprinted away from the screen, toward the gym's entrance. He brought her back, holding her arm high up in the air like he was announcing the winning contender in a boxing match.

"Welcome to the Grizzlies!" I said to her. Everyone cheered. Also, it's nice that Katarina is so cool with all this. I was kinda worried she would hate whoever came to the audition. But she's a good sport. Probably better than I would have been in her shoes. I guess I didn't really think about this before, but whether Katarina competes or not, now that Diane is part of the team, don't we need to work her into the routine either way? It wouldn't be fair to leave her out . . . would it? Must remember to discuss that with Jacqui next time we v-chat.

Ok, Dad just called to tell me there's some kind of hotel party going on downstairs. Going to go check out the free food!

GIVE ME A 125!

(LATE AT) NIGHT, MY VACATION CRIB

So, I **WAS** feeling pretty good about the
day after the Grizzly meeting:
I spoke to Evan (a little), my
team is safe and happy, **AND**
there was no one downstairs when
I went to check out the party
food—which meant I had
free reign over the best
snacks. Woot, woot!

Yum. cheese!

I booked it to the fancy
cheese plate and started
making myself a little brie and
cracker sandwich.

nom. nom nom

I must have been the first person on the scene,
because nothing had been touched. All the wineglasses
were lined up perfectly against the staircase—and
there was a bottle of wine that someone had just
opened but not poured. It started snowing outside
again, which made everything even cozier. But just as
I was relishing not being interrupted during my cheese
and snow reverie, a familiar voice called from the top
of the stairs.

"Ohmigod, Maddy, I had the <u>best</u> day!" squealed
Katie.

GIVE ME A
126!

I know I shouldn't be thinking this, but what kept
going through my head was: Katie's day just **HAD**
to be better than mine, didn't it? I tried to swat the
thought from my head and turned to face her. (I
was also desperately trying to talk without cracker
crumbs flying out of my mouth. Not so easy for me,
as we already know!) But she clearly wasn't paying any
attention as she bounded down the stairs toward me,
beaming.

"Hey," I said. "So the audition was good, I'm
guessing?"

"I totally killed the ballet portion," she said, one hand
on her hip. "I couldn't believe it!"

"That's great. Congrats!" And I really am happy for
her. Turns out this was a good day for auditions all
around ☺.

"Yeah, talking to you before really helped," she said,
as she made herself a cracker. "So thanks." She bit
into her cracker. "Mmmm. I love brie."

"You're welcome. And, yum, so do I." I smiled.

I decided I really like this version of Katie—the one
without Clementine and Hilary always strapped to each
side of her, sending bad vibes to all the people around
her. She just seems so much more . . . real. And **WAY**
less obnoxious.

GIVE ME A
127!

We hung out on the lobby couches, ignoring the slightly miffed stares of the hotel concierge as we stuffed our faces with cheese. We watched (and judged like they do on E!) as the other hotel guests arrived, most of them dressed up for a night out on the town. Then we played a game where we would make up stories about each guest and why they were there. It was totally something I'd do with Lanie.

"Nine o'clock," said Katie, without turning her head. "The woman in the red-and-black-striped dress. Don't be so obvious, Madison!"

"Ok," I said, turning my head toward Katie but sneaking glances in the woman's direction.

"All right," Katie continued. "Here's the story: This lady, she's totally a spy, pretending that she's here visiting her niece in the city. She's planted listening devices in all the rooms."

GIVE ME A 128!

"You're so wrong," I told her. "She's an old theater actress who lives in the hotel and imitates the personalities of the guests. She uses them for her performances."

"Hmmm," said Katie, thoughtfully placing a finger on her lips. "Could be. . . . So, what are your plans for tonight?"

"Um, spending more quality time with my dad and his girlfriend. What else would I be doing?"

Katie's eyes had a mischievous gleam to them. "Well, my mom said I could hang out with some of the kids I met at auditions. She has some party to go to that will totally be boring. But these girls I met invited me to go to the planetarium to see a light show. You wanna come?"

I thought about my two options.

1) Nerding out with Dad and Beth and singing "New York, New York," (it's become this new pastime of theirs since we got here) as we walked down Broadway.

2) Meeting some real NYC kids and seeing my first laser light show.

Hmm . . . tough decision, huh? Ha-ha. Too bad Dad would so **NOT** go for it in a million years.

"Thanks for the invite," I told her. "But my dad is definitely not going to let me go out alone in the city." I shook my head.

GIVE ME A 129!

"Duh, don't tell him we're alone. Just tell him you're going out to dinner with my mom and me. I'm sure he'd like some alone time with his girlfriend. Right?"

At first I was thinking, not a bad plan! Then I thought some more.

"What if he talks to your mom?"

"Chill. I'll distract her," Katie said with a sly smile.

I felt bad about lying to my dad—but then I realized, he kind of lied to me, too. He brought me on this trip pretending this was just a "last-minute vacation." And it so wasn't. I mean, how long has he known he's moving to New York? Nice of him to wait and tell me at the last minute. I wouldn't be surprised if he's having moving boxes shipped here by the end of the week. Besides, it's not like Katie's new friends were going somewhere dangerous or anything—it was just the planetarium. I figured the worst that could happen was that I'd get neck pains from looking up at the screen overhead. And anyway, supposedly it was just up the block. So I decided: Might as well let Dad get used to his new life in the city. After all, this is what city kids do. And he wanted me to be a city kid, didn't he?? (I also had a feeling he'd say yes, since he probably still felt bad about our tiff yesterday.)

I popped the question to Dad when he and Beth were drinking some vino.

GIVE ME A
130!

"Sure," he said. "If that's what you want. But I'd like to talk to Katie's mother first."

"Oh, right," said Katie, as innocent as an angel. "She's showering upstairs. Do you want me to go get her?"

Katie was good. It was a perfect excuse to not have the parental units talk to each other. I knew my dad would feel awkward about interrupting someone while they were getting ready—especially a woman. Also, he didn't have any reason to think I wasn't telling the truth. In my whole life I've never given him a reason not to trust me. I'm not the lying daughter type. Or at least I **WASN'T** the lying daughter type.

"Hmm . . . well," said Dad. "We do have to get moving soon to make it in time for our reservation." He gave me a worried look. "Promise you'll stick close to Katie's mom, ok?"

"Ooookay, Dad. I'm not a little girl."

"Yeah, yeah. But you're my little girl, so be safe."

Mega embarrassing! He might as well have put a little bow on my head and pinched my cheek.

At least Dad believed me. Kinda crazy how easy it was. . . .

I went back upstairs to change. When I got to my room, I noticed someone had dropped what looked like room service menus under my door. Hmm, that would

GIVE ME A 13!!

be fancy! I bent down to see what they were and realized they weren't menus at all—they were pamphlets for different art schools that Dad has been researching for me. I suddenly felt all warm and fuzzy inside.

Warm & fuzzy

Maybe Dad really is serious about me coming here. He seems to be trying to give me a lot of reasons to consider it. I put the pamphlets aside so I could read them later. I had bigger problems at hand right at that moment: what to wear when hanging out with real city kids?

It took me **FOREVER** to decide, because I knew the look would have to be just right. First I tried on some skinny jeans with an oversize sweater and lots of bracelets. Nah. Too much like a little kid wearing her dad's sweater. Next I tried on jean shorts with tights and boots.

GIVE ME A 132!

Too Madonna circa the superolden days. Finally I decided on a tank top under a blazer with black pants. And my **NEW BOOTS**! It was absolute perfection!

Dad and Beth had already left for dinner by the time I met Katie downstairs. We were in the clear. Freeeedoooom! I could hardly believe it was happening to me. Lanie is going to **FLIP** out when I tell her (and not just because of the Katie factor). And the most awesome thing about New York is you totally don't have to be able to drive to get around. So much is just within easy walking distance. And if not? There's tons of public transportation (note my subway experience in previous entries), not to mention, like, a bazillion cabs all over the place.

"So your mom is cool with you going out alone?" I asked, as we walked off into the freezing cold night.

GIVE ME A 133!

"Negative," she said, shaking her head. "She'd kill me if she knew I was out without a chaperone. I told her I was going to one of my dance friends' houses around the corner. She was so proud of my audition today, she didn't give me a hassle at all."

Katie gave me the lowdown on the girls we were going to meet as we walked up Central Park West. "This isn't the typical New York City private school prep crowd, if that's what you're expecting," she explained. "They're a little more artsy. A little more out there."

I laughed. "I'm having a little trouble picturing <u>you</u> with artsy-looking friends."

Katie smiled. "I know, I know. They're no Clementines and Hilarys. But that's what I kind of like about 'em. And besides, I wouldn't be able to chill with these kinds of kids back in Port Angeles. No one would get it."

I shrugged. She was probably right.

When we got to the lobby of the planetarium, I noticed that Katie's friends all kind of looked like Lanie, but slightly more put together. This **WAS** total artsy crowd central.

I stood around awkwardly as Katie hugged everyone hello.

"Hey, I'm Magda," said one of the ballerinas when she noticed me on the sidelines.

GIVE ME A
134!

"Oh. Sorry. This is my friend Madison," said Katie. "From home."

What a bizarre moment. Katie introducing me as "her friend." Right?

"Hey, I'm Penelope," said another girl. She was tall and had a really long neck. She reminded me of a really beautiful giraffe.

Penelope and Magda brought some other friends along too: This guy Luc, who was a total goofball, another guy named Darren, who also was a ballet dancer, and Cynthia, a friend from Magda's building. It was cool to be alone and out and about in New York. I mean, it's not like Mom follows me around every time I go out with a friend in Port Angeles, but we always go to places right in town: the coffee shop, the pizza place, the movies. And our town isn't that big. In fact, probably the entire population of my town could fit in my teeny, tiny hotel room. These kids are my age, but they seem at least five years older from the way they talk to each other and how comfortable they are just hanging out in the city without parents. Maybe this is how it is for city kids—total freedom, you know? I could **DEFINITELY** get used to that.

At the laser light show, I ended up sitting next to Luc (who BTW is ah-dorable-looking). He has this really

GIVE ME A
135!

cute jet-black hair, which he wore parted in the middle and shaved on one side. I'd never seen a kid with hair like that in Port Angeles. He had on this really old-looking sweater with holes in it that looked like it was from a vintage store. And he wore combat boots—which I've

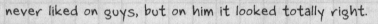

never liked on guys, but on him it looked totally right.

I'm pretty positive that someone like Luc could stop Lanie's Dustin Barker crush any day. The weird thing was? I was kind of crushing on him all night! Not in, like, a serious way. Nothing like the Bevan thing. Just, like, in a can't-stop-staring-at-him way.

He kept on cracking corny jokes all throughout the light show, whispering in my ear and imitating the sophisticated British voice of the narrator.

"So are you into acting or something?" I asked him, since he had that outgoing performance vibe, like Jared's drama friends.

"I've been in a couple of my friends' projects for school," he said. "But I'm more into making things. I do abstract portraits of my friends. Like floating heads and stuff."

GIVE ME A 136!

Floating heads? Oookaay.

"What's your deal? You a dancer or something?" he asked me.

"Nope." I laughed. "Cheerleader, actually." I felt a little embarrassed about it for some reason. Like I should be doing something cooler or more sophisticated. (And now I feel totally bad about that, too. Why was I embarrassed? I know cheerleading is a highly athletic sport, and that it takes a lot of skill and dedication. How can I be so insecure that a couple of out-there artistic kids made me doubt that?)

"No way. You? A cheer head?"

"Hey. It's not like that."

I wish I had told him how totally awesome cheerleading is and how dedicated you have to be to succeed. But I didn't.

"Suuuure," he said, shaking his head and smiling.

"I also design my own clothes," I pointed out.

"That's cool," he said, nodding approvingly. He gaze went from my shoes to my head. "You wearing any of your work?"

"Actually, yeah. This top." I showed him the tank, which I had ripped up from a long T-shirt and sewed together with lace and safety pins.

Someone leaned in behind me and whispered, "shhhhh!

GIVE ME A 137!

keep it down in front, please. **SHEESH!**"

We looked at each other and laughed.

Afterward, we all went to this famous pizza parlor and got a huge table. I looked to my right, and there was Luc, holding a menu open. How'd that happen? I looked across the table, and Katie gave me a wink. Like she was saying, "Ahh, so what's going on with you two?" (Which, PS, is totally weird because she **OBVI** knows about me and Bevan.)

"No!" I mouthed to her silently. For, like, three seconds I wondered if she just wanted to make me think she was ok with me flirting with Luc, but the second we got back home she was going to spill the beans to Bevan. But she wouldn't do that . . . right? Not after she confided in me about dance and all. I mean, I have dirt on her. I'm safe. Aren't I?? Anyway, I quickly realized I shouldn't be flirting with Luc. I like Bevan. Period.

Still, we ended up having such a blast together. It was weird how easy it was to talk to him and make him laugh. And I don't know why, but he made me feel more comfortable around all of Katie's friends. Like I wasn't some outsider.

"Hey, you guys," Luc said, addressing the table once everyone got their pizzas. "Maddy here is a fashion designer."

GIVE ME A 138!

"Oh, please," I said. "I make some of my own clothes. But I'm not, like, serious or anything."

"She made the top she's wearing right now," he said, biting into a slice.

"Wow, that's so rad," said Cynthia. "I make jewelry."

Rad? That's **SO** the kind of word an artsy, independent city kid would use. It's like their DNA is just cooler. Sigh.

"Really?" I said. "Cool."

Cynthia leaned over the table so she could show me her bracelets. "I take a metalworking class downtown and make them from scratch."

That's when I realized it was the first time I was actually happy to not be thought of as a cheerleader. To this crowd, I was an artist—like them. And I **REALLY** liked the feeling of being part of the group, of having some talent to contribute, you know? The more time I spent with them, the more I realized the dilemma Katie is going through. From the second you get involved in the cheerleading thing it becomes your life. And a big part of me loves that . . . but it was also really nice to be seen as, well, something other than a cheerleader. But it's hard to do that at home. I get so swept up in the Grizzlies, just like Katie gets swept up in the Titans, and it's like people in cheer expect us to

GIVE ME A
139!

be all about cheer all the time—and nothing else. Like we're not allowed to have other interests. Double sigh.

Anyway, after dinner, we all walked over to Penelope's apartment. Which was the only truthful part of tonight's plan that Katie had told her mom about. Except, of course, that Penelope's parents weren't home. "Yeah, my mom would definitely not have been cool with this," whispered Katie, as we walked to Penelope's.

Oh, by the way? Her apartment was AMAZING. It was in a super-old building and had multiple "wings." Penelope warned us not to go past the big hallway that separated her room, the TV room, and the kitchen from the rest of the apartment.

"My parents have, like, this sixth sense when it comes to me having my friends over," she explained. "They're so freaked out about people ruining their furniture, they make Esme clean everything from top to bottom every time, like, one person comes to visit."

(PS—Esme is their live-in maid. Guess these kids were more like private school kids than Katie thought.)

We hung out in Penelope's room for a bit, and then watched a movie. Halfway through, I left to go to the bathroom (just one of the eight—yup, EIGHT—bathrooms in the apartment), and when I came out, Luc was leaning against the wall in the hallway, checking his messages.

GIVE ME A 140!

"Bad reception in there," he said, motioning to his phone and then to the den. "So, you like the movie so far?"

"It's ok." I shrugged. "Not so into subtitles."

"Yeah." He laughed. "Me neither."

I'm pretty glad I wasn't the only one. "Hard to read in the dark," I added.

"Good point."

We ended up hanging in the kitchen and just talking about everything: our favorite music, some of the art I've seen this week, and even fashion. I could never imagine talking about this stuff with Bevan. It just isn't really his style. I mean, Bevan is funny and sweet and all, but our conversations usually center around school, cheer, soccer, and friends. We don't really talk about books or movies or stuff like that. That is definitely more like Evan's and my convos.

Penelope came into the kitchen to make some popcorn for everyone. Luc picked up the comic book that was lying on the counter next to some magazines.

"Be careful with that," said Penelope. "My brother will massacre you if you bend the pages." She rolled her eyes.

Ha-ha. Her bro sounded so much like someone else I know. . . .

Luc smiled. "Don't worry. Me and comic books have

GIVE ME A 14!!

a thing for one another," he joked. "I'll be gentle." As I watched him flip through the pages, it hit me: Not only did Luc seem to be the total opposite of Bevan, but also he **REALLY** reminded me of Evan. If Evan, um, wore combat boots and had a crazy half-weird, half-cool haircut.

But I must have been imagining things. Because if Evan and Luc were as similar as I was thinking they were, and I was kind of crushing on Luc, that would mean . . . uh-uh. No way!! That would mean that . . . I could actually fall for a guy like Evan? Like there's something I'm looking for in a guy that Evan has and Bevan doesn't. Which is **RIDICULOUS**! Besides, this is nuts. It's vacation. I shouldn't be thinking so hard or looking into things so much. Evan is my friend. Luc is just some cute guy I met. And Bevan is the guy I **LIKE**. Right? (One last thing, though: suspicious that the name Bevan is just Evan with a B??? Why has this never occurred to me before?? Boy, I must be crazy. Seriously loco.)

But back to the night in question . . . So, Luc and I lost track of time, chatting away in the kitchen until I happened to glance at the huge grandfather clock in Penelope's hallway.

"Ohmigod! Is it really this late?" I asked. I ran to

GIVE ME A
142!

the den, where Katie had fallen asleep during the movie with popcorn all over her lap. I bent down to nudge her awake. "Katie, my dad is going to flip out!"

Katie looked startled, like she didn't know where she was. Then she looked at her watch. "Oh, no. I told my mom I'd call her from the hotel at ten—and she has caller ID. We need to get back, Madison."

Luc seemed a little sad that I was going. "You're a cool chick, Madison. I wish we could have hung out longer," he said, leaning casually against the door to the apartment as I put my shoes on. "I'll e-mail you."

Sweet! The little butterflies in my tummy were fluttering a mile a minute. I know I wasn't really supposed to be interested, or whatever, but it's nice to be liked, right?? Who doesn't like that!? I wanted to be all chill and relaxed, and be like, "Sure, whatever."

Instead I just stammered, "I uh . . . Cool. Ok!" Typical Maddy.

The thing is, I do kind of wish we had more time together. But liking multiple guys is so **NOT** a Maddy thing to do. (And T.G. Katie hadn't been there at that moment to overhear what he said. I know we're supposedly friends now, but I'm still playing it safe. At least for now.)

On our super-hurried walk back, the conversation

GIVE ME A 143!

did a total 180. Katie was going on and on about getting into the academy. "Of course, if I get in, I'll need to replace myself as Titan captain."

I didn't know a single cheerleader who was good enough to replace Katie as captain. (Except for maybe Jacqui, but there isn't a chance of that happening.)

But then she said something completely ridiculous. "I could train you to replace me." I stopped dead in my tracks, and my mouth fell open in this look of complete and utter shock—like I was witnessing zombies pop out of fresh graves.

Razzmatazz!

Finally, I choked out the words, "Excuse me?" Then I literally looked behind me, because the next thought that occurred to me was that someone like Hilary or Clementine had just magically appeared.

GIVE ME A 144!

"I know, I know. It will take tons of work—believe me—but I've seen you. You're better than you know. If someone pushed you to train even harder than you do now—like <u>really</u> pushed you, you totally could be Titan captain material. It's just, you're spending so much of your energy on your team right now, you don't have enough time to focus on yourself, to push yourself to the next level. Don't get me wrong, you're a good captain and you're doing what a good captain does: putting the team first. But if you could just focus on improving your own skills, you could really kill out there."

My brain turned to mush for a second while it processed this. I mean, this talk was completely astronomical. First of all, Katie sort of gave **ME** the chance to be a **TITAN**. (Uh, hello, Madison Hays? This is your lifelong dream calling!) And second, she said she wants to train me to be a **CAPTAIN** on top of that? Is there some little cheerleading Fairy Godmother who's suddenly decided to show up and make my life absolutely perfect?

Rah, rah, rah!

Sis—Boom—Bah!

GIVE ME A 145!

I kept waiting for Katie to just burst out into hysterical laughter and be like, "Just kidding!" But she didn't. She was serious. She IS serious.

"But what about the other girls on your squad?" I asked. "I'm sure you have lots of captain wannabes."

Katie slowed down as we approached the hotel. "Yeah, there are girls who are good, but I don't think anyone on the team really has what it takes to lead the pack. You know? Like, they can cheer really well—but captain material? No one makes the cut."

"So what, you can just nominate me, and that's it?" I asked incredulously.

"No." She shook her head. "It's a vote. But," she said, with a smug smile, "the team always ends up following the captain's lead. If I vote for you, they will too."

"Must be nice, having a team that actually listens to you," I mumbled under my breath, but she didn't acknowledge having heard me.

Her teeth looked so white; they practically glowed in the dark as we stood across from each other under the streetlights. "I mean, you'll have to make the team first, but there's another round of tryouts in the spring. If you train with me, I can get you ready."

I tried to absorb all this, but it's a lot to take in! Finally we came up to the steps of the hotel. The

GIVE ME A
146!

old-fashioned lamps over the main entrance cast an eerie glow over Katie.

"But remember what I told you earlier," she said, all traces of a smile gone from her face. "If you become a Titan, you can't even think about doing anything else in your life. The Titans become your life."

I feel like the Grizzlies have **ALREADY** taken over my life. I can't even imagine how it is with the Titans. But we've all heard the stories. . . . That must be a big part of why Katie wants to leave cheerleading. She must be fed up with the Titans being the be-all and end-all.

"Wait—so this is why you want to come to New York, right? To get away from all of it?" I asked.

"Partly," she said. "But it's also that I need to prove to myself that I am not just one thing. I love cheer, but it is not the only thing I love. And no one sees me as anything but a cheerleader."

It was almost like she had been reading my mind. That was exactly how I was feeling all night long. And I guess it isn't just Katie and me—there's Diane Huerta, too. She loves to dance and do gymnastics, but because she's in drama club, everyone thinks she's just a drama geek. Why do we create these tiny little boxes that we can't escape from? And what's worse, why do we let

GIVE ME A 147!

people put us in them in the first place??

When we were inside the hotel library, Katie called her mom from the hotel phone to tell her we were back and safe. Then she insisted on teaching me some Titan moves. "Just in case you need a reminder about why the Titans are the best," she said confidently. "Also, for some reason, cheering always helps with my pre-performance jitters. And tomorrow's the modern dance audition."

I was psyched. I hadn't done anything cheer related all week except some stretches in my room. Luckily, the couches were still up against the wall where they had been placed for the hotel party earlier. The library suddenly turned into a perfect practice space for us! We couldn't do anything too, too crazy, but Katie showed me her standing back tuck—which is a killer move that I'm still working on—and she gave me some pointers. It's super tough because you have to be able to do a backflip from a standing position, which means zero momentum helping you get around.

I had just nearly landed it when Dad burst into the room. And he didn't look happy.

"Madison Jane Hays," he said, in a measured but serious tone. "I need to talk to you right now. In private."

GIVE ME A 148!

Katie made a face like, "Yikes. I'm glad I'm not you right now."

I waved good-bye to her and followed Dad to my room. I didn't need an audience in front of me while Daddy-O ripped me apart.

As soon as he shut the door to my room behind him, he asked, "Do you want to know who I ran into just now?"

"Um . . ." I stalled, bending down to take my boots off.

"Katie's mother. And she told me that she was just at a party—without Katie. Without you. So," he said, crossing his arms over his chest, "if you weren't with Mrs. Parker, where in the world were you?"

The first thought in my head was whether Dad had blabbed to Katie's mom about our lie. "Did you tell on Katie?" I asked.

He shook his head no. Props to Dad. "But believe me, her mom is good and angry."

I fessed up and told him about the whole night.

"What were you thinking, going out by yourself? And lying to me about it?" he demanded, when I was done telling him what happened.

All of my anger and pent-up frustration about my dad moving away to NYC came out suddenly in one big angry rush.

GIVE ME A 149!

"Dad, I'm not a little girl. Please stop treating me like one! It's not like you're Mr. Perfect. You're, like, never around when we're at home. You take me out to dinner, like, once a month, and then get annoyed that I'm not posh enough for the places you take me. When you call me on the phone, all you do is try to convince me to quit cheer. And then you take me on vacation and start acting like you're this responsible dad all of a sudden. Tell me honestly, how long have you been keeping this move a secret from me?"

"Madison, I—"

"No, seriously. Did you really think I'd buy this as a last-minute offer, the way I bought this last-minute vacation? I'm not about to fall for the same trick twice."

"Madison, it's not like that. Ok, yes, I've known for a little while, but it wasn't like I wanted to keep it from you. I . . . we—"

"I hope you enjoy New York City, because don't even think I'll visit you here, let alone live with you."

Ok, so that was not true—but I was super mad!

Dad was silent for a few moments. I noticed for the first time tonight that he looked tired. I guess worrying about the whereabouts of your only child does that to you.

GIVE ME A 150!

"Madison, we didn't want to tell you about the move until you'd had a chance to see the city a little." He looked down at his feet. "But you're right. We should have told you earlier, and we never should have sprung this trip on you as just a regular vacation." He sighed. "That wasn't fair, and I'm sorry we put this on you all at once. And I realize that I'm not always around at home when you need me, but the best I can say is, I'm trying to improve that. That's why I asked you about living with us."

He apologized! My dad! Totally didn't expect that. Not that I'm doubting myself or anything. I am totally right. But still, it was really nice to hear. "I'm sorry, Dad. It's just going to take some getting used to. Maybe we can just call us even now?"

Dad laughed. "Sure, Madison." He held out his hand so we could shake on it. "Only if you promise never to lie to me again."

"Deal." And I meant it.

"In that case, we're even."

After he left, I picked up some of the brochures he'd left me before. One brochure showed a montage of students dancing, sketching, and acting in a play. A total artsy school. I never really penned myself for "one of those kinds of kids." But I guess I kind of am,

GIVE ME A 15!!

if I really think about it. Ha! I'm more like Lanie than I ever thought.

I'm actually starting to imagine what it would be like to go to school here in the city. Instead of being driven in a car to get to school, or walking along the suburban streets, I'd take a subway. And instead of going to the **ONE** coffee shop in town, I'd have my pick: starbucks, no-name cafés, diners . . . And my group of friends? It would be a crazy talented group, like the kids from tonight, and each person would do something totally amazing in the arts. We'd go to cool shows and art exhibits, and check out stores together. It would be insane!

GIVE ME A 152!

That's when my phone rang: Bevan. I instantly felt guilty about having hung out with Luc. Which is silly because it's not like anything happened. But still . . .

"Hey, Mads! Haven't heard from you in a while," he said.

"Oh, yeah," I said, suddenly feeling even more guilty for not being in touch with him more. "It's been super busy here. We've just been doing a million things."

"That's cool," he said. I could hear one of his favorite bands playing over his iPod speakers in the background. "Have you just been chilling with your parents? Or have you met any city kids?"

In a perfect world, I would have poured my heart out to Bevan about all that was happening, and he totally could have helped me work through it. I mean, isn't that what's supposed to happen when two people like each other? They talk about important things and care about each other's opinions and stuff? But I didn't. He just wouldn't have gotten it. Not like Lanie . . . or Evan.

"Actually," I said. "I hung out with a group of dancers that Katie is friends with."

"Katie?" he asked, confusion in his voice.

OOPS. Ruh-roh.

"Oh. Uh. Oh, man. I actually wasn't supposed to say

GIVE ME A
153!

anything. But can you keep a secret?"

"Of course," he said.

"Katie Parker is here, in New York City, auditioning for a spot in a dance program here. It is mega competitive."

"You're serious?" he asked.

"Yeah, but you really, really cannot tell a soul. This can't get back to the Titans. I can't believe I just slipped!"

"No worries. I'm good with secrets. Besides, none of my friends would care, anyway. So, were you hanging out with, like, ballerinas?"

"Well, yeah. There were ballerinas, and some other friends of theirs."

He was silent for a few moments.

"Any guys?"

It was so weird. I've never heard him be jealous before. And never in a million years would I have guessed that **THE** Bevan Ramsey would be jealous of little ol' me hanging out with other guys.

"Yeah, a couple," I told him, trying to be casual about it. "They were nice, though."

I don't know why, but I felt like I was hiding something from him.

"Oh," said Bevan. "Cool."

GIVE ME A
154!

"Anyway," I said. "You'd love this hotel. It's super old, and there are some pretty crazy characters here." I thought of telling him about the game Katie and I had played earlier when we were in the lobby, but worried he'd think it was stupid.

"Ha. Cool. Hey, I miss you."

It was such a sweet thing to say. My heart should have melted right then and there. Rewind to just over a week ago, and I would have been attempting somersaults of joy in my room. But something felt a little off.

"Awww," was all I could manage. "Well, I wish I could talk more, but I have to get to bed. We have an early morning tomorrow."

"Skating in Rockefeller Center?" he asked.

"That'll probably happen at some point, but no. First Chinatown," I told him.

"Ooh. Make sure to eat some dumplings for me."

"I will!" I said. "G'night."

"Sweet dreams."

I know I should be missing him more right now, but for some reason, all I can think about is Evan and how quiet he's been. I kind of expected some sort of message from him later today. But—nothing! The boy is incommunicado. Is it just that I'm not used to him

GIVE ME A 155!

ignoring me that it's become this big thing? And this whole Luc-reminding-me-of-Evan thing is just so weird. I mean, here I am all the way in New Year—all the way on the other side of the COUNTRY—and the guy I'm supposed to like just told me he misses me and I feel nothing except the strange and sudden urge to get off the phone. YET, all I CAN think about are: A) some boy who's like Evan's slightly cooler twin brother and, B) the fact that Evan-in-the-flesh won't message me!!!!

Grrr. Where is my fairy godmother when I need her?? ☹.

GIVE ME A 156!

Friday, January 6

Night, chillin' on the comfy couches

Spirit Level:

Fashionably Frosty

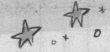

What a totally crazy day! It's really incredible how everything just keeps moving here, like, at a mile-a-minute speed, and it's so easy to get wrapped up in it. The speed of Port Angeles after this is going to be, like, a major letdown.

So, this morning we went for a walk through Chinatown. Beth is totally tea-obsessed, so we went into a store she'd heard about that sells all kinds of weird teas. Dad chose this one tea called "gunpowder tea." Yuck! It smelled like gym socks. I was like, "Yeah, Dad. Hey-none for me, thanks. But enjoy."

GIVE ME A 157!

It was below freezing, though, so every few minutes we'd have to find an excuse to go inside a store. The highlight of the morning was definitely this little cart on the side of the road that made mini pancakes—practically doll-size. The old woman making them filled a wax paper bag to the brim with the little dough rounds, and it only cost two dollars!!! Also, I don't know how anyone figures out the streets downtown, because I would be completely lost if I lived there. Each street zigzags into another, and before you know it, you're in a dead end.

Dad found a cute French restaurant downtown where we had delish eggs Benedict and fluffy waffles. And just as we were finishing up, who walked in but Daphne Song—one of **THE** biggest fashion bloggers in New York. Who else could make bundling up in the freezing cold look so good?

She practically discovered the Draper sisters—these amazingly cool designers (who are actually real sisters!) who are known for taking ripped and tattered fabrics and putting them together into unique pieces. When I'm a gazillionaire, I'm totally going to buy something of theirs ☺. Once you have the Daphne Seal of Approval, you're pretty much on the path to becoming the next "It" designer. OMG, Life Dream

GIVE ME A 158!

Numero Dos (or is it Uno???).

So get this: Daphne sat right across from us and began playing with her camera. It would have been so cool if she took a pic of us, but what were the chances of that happening? I'm clearly not a celebrity or model or anything. Still, a girl can dream. I must have been drooling over her rockin' outfit, because I heard Dad clear his throat a couple of times. (He does that to get my attention.)

"Is that some sort of celebrity?" Beth asked.

"Well, to me she is," I said. "She's a fashion blogger."

Dad raised an eyebrow. "Is that even a job?"

"Yeah," I said. "She gets paid in free clothes, I guess."

Sidebar: I actually have no idea how fashion bloggers make money, but when the top designers send you all

GIVE ME A 159!

that free stuff so you can critique them, what else do you need?

I told them that Daphne has made a lot of designers super famous. Like the Draper sisters. And surprisingly Beth actually knew who they were! Major points for Beth. It pains me to say this . . . **BUT** . . . my opinion of her is totally shifting—strictly in the fashion arena, that is.

"Do <u>you</u> have a blog, Madison?" asked Beth.

I laughed and shook my head. "Not yet," I said. "But I do have a ton of my own designs and love putting together looks from different ads in magazines."

"Madison, remember that dress you were in love with when you were five?" Dad added, trying to join in on the conversation. "The one Grandma bought you with all the bows?"

"Ohmigod, I looooooooved that dress."

"You wore it every day, until the seams came apart." He chuckled to himself at the memory.

GIVE ME A
160!

"I guess I've loved fashion since I could walk, huh?" About as long as I've loved cheer.

Dad nodded. "Maybe you'd like to research some of the schools in the pamphlets I gave you? We could do it together this afternoon, even."

I could tell he was trying to be casual about the question—so that I wouldn't think he was trying to force me into anything.

Beth patted Dad on the arm reassuringly. "As you know, Madison, there's no better place to learn all about fashion than New York," she said.

A part of me is still a little annoyed that Dad is so over the moon about taking me away from my cheer life. But then, maybe he just wants to give me a chance to do something **ELSE** I love.

I looked back at Daphne. A woman (who definitely could have been a model) tapped her on the shoulder and gave her two air kisses. Daphne showed her some of the pics on her camera, and the two of them laughed about something. As I looked at her in all her fabulousness, I realized, hey, that could be me someday! The thing is, I think I have to give some real thought to Dad's offer. . . . What if coming here to study fashion and art is this once-in-a-lifetime opportunity? Mom even said it herself, there's more to life than

GIVE ME A 16!!

cheer. **AND**, at some point cheer has to end. What happens then?

As if I need more drama. Let's take a look at the long list of things bugging me on this vacay, shall we??

1) There's the Bevan/Evan debate
2) There's the weird Luc attraction
3) There's Katarina vs. "the social studies" and subsequently, Get Up and Cheer
4) AND there's the whole Katie-wants-me-to-take-her-Titan-captain-throne thing

Yes, I'd say piling on a "to move or not to move" question is **EXACTLY** what I need right now.

I noticed that as the day went on, I was already starting to feel better about Dad moving to New York. The thought crossed my mind that a big part of why he invited me on this trip was because he was feeling guilty about moving away. Like taking me to NYC would make up for it. But I don't think that's the reason anymore. It seems like he really does want me to be a part of his life here, and isn't just saying stuff about me going to school here because he has to. For the first time in, like, ever, Dad seems to care about my designing thing and isn't trying to convince me to take

GIVE ME A 162!

classes on how to be an astronaut or something like that. It's kinda nice. Actually, it's more than nice.

"I'd kinda like to see FIT. Just to see what my potential future could be like," I said, even though I can hardly wrap my head around me being a college student one day. Eek!

Dad smiled, and it felt good to know I'd made him happy ☺.

Anyway, I called Jacqui today to see how practice was going with the new chick. "Diane's doing really great!" said Jacqui. "Higher, guys!" she barked into the phone, obviously talking to the squad.

"Everyone likes her," continued Jacqui. "And she's catching on so quickly. She's already learned the new routine, and now we're working on some pyramid stuff. This girl is strong!"

"You have her doing pyramid stunts? Already?" I knew Diane was good from the tryouts, but this all seemed a little fast.

"Trust me. She's up to it," Jacqui said.

Jacqui knows what she's doing, so I guess I have to trust her. "So, what about Katarina?" I asked.

According to Jacqui, Katarina has memorized all the main ideas from the chapters that will be covered on her test. Matt taught her some mnemonic devices to

GIVE ME A
163!

Tell me everything you know about the Civil War or give me twenty!

remember everything. He also has her do sit-ups whenever she gets something wrong. (I wonder who he picked that one up from . . . ahem, Jacqui!) By the end of their tutoring session, she was so sore she refused to miss an answer.

It was reassuring to hear that there's hope for Katarina. But then I started worrying about what would happen if she passes. "So what will we do with Diane?" I asked Jacqui.

"Um," Jacqui paused. "Well, we can always use another teammate—especially a good one. It won't be so hard to add another girl into the routine, and having another girl who can do stunts and tumble will actually give us a much better shot at winning."

"Sounds like you've got it all under control!" I answered.

It'll definitely be weird to have a new member on the team. I feel like we've all become this close little

GIVE ME A 164!

family. Will things change with someone new in the mix? I mean, I guess Diane, who already has flying skills, will probably change things for the better when it comes to us competing, like Jacqui said. But still—I kind of like things just the way they were. (Funny for me to say, I know, since I'm considering leaving the team completely.)

As I listened over the phone to the sounds of everyone practicing in the gym, I really started to miss my teammates. Thinking about Jared's goofy dance routines, and Ian and Matt's antics, got me a little misty eyed, I have to say. How will I handle it if I move to New York and never get to cheer with them again? Or worse, if I stay but make the Titan team? So much is going through my head right now, I literally have no idea what to do. I wish I could at least talk to Mom about this, but she doesn't know about New York yet. And anyway, I'm pretty sure I know what her opinion on that will be. Also, being the Grizzly coach means she's kind of biased on the Grizzly vs. Titan issue as well. The only totally impartial person is probably Lanes. T.G. I have her.

Later this afternoon, we took a walk through the Garment District, which I'd been waiting to see all week. It's only **THE** fashion capital for the biggest designers and couture houses. I think I expected

GIVE ME A 165!

everyone there to look like they just walked out of a magazine. Instead there were lots of girls walking around in homemade-looking clothes, carrying giant sketchbooks and bags of fabric. The Fashion Institute of Technology was not that far from where we were, so I figured that's where these girls were coming from and going to. We hung out on the steps of one of the buildings for a while and watched the fashionable girls come and go. Then we looked for some of the famous showrooms that were supposed to be in the area but didn't find them. I took a picture of the street sign that said "Fashion Avenue." I'm going to blow it up, frame it, and hang it up. (Hurrah! for homemade art. I feel like one of those interior designers on some home makeover show.)

"So, Madison, can you imagine living on Fashion Ave someday?" asked Beth.

"That would be ah-mazing!" I said, laughing. "But until then, it can just hang on my wall at home."

When we got back to the hotel, I called Katie's room to see how her second audition went.

GIVE ME A
166!

"Not so good," said Katie glumly. "I think I messed up by not getting a good night's sleep last night. I just wasn't able to give it 120%."

"I'm sorry, Katie," I said.

"It's not your fault," she said. "The whole thing was my idea—going out with my friends the night before a big audition. And modern was supposed to be the easy part! I mean, what was I thinking—seriously? I don't know how I managed to lose track of time last night. I should have gone to bed way earlier. Anyway, I just hope my other audition gets taken into consideration. I killed that one."

"I'm sure you didn't do as badly as you think you did," I said, trying to reassure her. Knowing Katie, her idea of "bad" was another person's idea of more than perfect.

"Well, whatever," said Katie. "My mom is taking me out to this famous ice cream place called Serendipity to cheer me up. You wanna come with? This time I'll actually ask her to talk to your dad for real."

"Sounds fun," I agreed.

I still can't get over the fact that Katie and I actually have a friend thing going on. I never would have imagined—especially after what happened when Bevan started liking me, and my huge fight with her

GIVE ME A
167!

at Regionals. It's been nice hanging out with her, but I wonder what it will be like when we go home. I mean, it's pretty clear that she can't really be all buddy-buddy with me around Clementine. Hilary is easily swayed. (I mean, the girl is so gullible she thought Jacqui's addition of shoulder pads to my original Titan design was retro, ha-ha!) Still, it's definitely going to be interesting. Good thing I don't have to worry about it until I get home!

Dad agreed to let me go with Mrs. Parker (this time he insisted on talking to her face-to-face). The place? Was the **COOLEST**!! I was thinking we were just going to go to some boring ice cream parlor, but as soon as we got there, there was a line out the door. (How could I think for one minute that Katie Parker would go somewhere boring? Silly Madison.) Obviously, Katie would know about the "it" ice cream place ☺.

Luckily, we only had to wait twenty minutes. Inside, they have this adorable general store where you can buy teddy bears, hot chocolate, or these really cool old-fashioned lamps. And the desserts there are so amazing!! Their famous frozen hot chocolate comes in a glass so big, you could literally stick your entire face in it. You wouldn't, of course, because that would be gross and messy. But that's

GIVE ME A 168!

how big it is. Katie and I ended up sharing that one. At one point she thought it would be really funny to launch a whipped cream blob onto my face.

I didn't think it was that funny, but then Katie took one look at my face and completely lost it. At least she wasn't feeling so miserable anymore. Who knew that food all over my face would one day be a good thing??!

On our way back from Serendipity, Katie asked if I wanted to have another cheer lesson when we got back to the hotel. I never say no to an opportunity to cheer with a Titan. . . .

This time we had to move the couches in the hotel library on our own. Thankfully, none of the staff was really around to notice or give us a hard time about it.

"So, have you given any thought to what I said the other day?" asked Katie, while we warmed up. "Do you want me to train you for Titan tryouts this spring?"

"I—I don't know, Katie," I stuttered. It's the truth. I don't know what I want.

"I'm pretty confused about a lot of things right

GIVE ME A
169!

now. I can't believe I'm saying this, but I really like being a Grizzly."

"But haven't you always wanted to be a Titan?" she looked at me as if I'd just told her I preferred spinach quiche over a double fudge sundae.

"I know! I did," I said. "But the Grizzlies are . . . well, they're family now. I'm not saying I've made my final decision or anything. It would be amazing to be a Titan—especially a captain."

"Yeah, obviously."

"Well, we can still train together, without me having to make a decision just yet, can't we?"

Katie shrugged. "Sure, if that's what you want. Anyways, I guess I should wait and see if I actually get into this school before I start planning my departure from the team and your future as team captain."

We did a ton of stretching, and then Katie showed me how to take my scorpion to the next level. I already know I'm going to be mega sore tomorrow. Which is a good thing—besides these little practice sessions with Katie, I haven't been doing a ton of cheer stuff this week.

When we were done, I saw that I had a missed call from Evan. Yay! Finally!

He hadn't called me all week before this. I hate

GIVE ME A 170!

being the only one making an effort. He didn't leave me a message, which is totally annoying. But I forgive him. In fact, I'm actually a little nervous about calling him back. Weird, right? I mean, it's just Evan. Dorky, comic-book-loving, messy-haired, sarcastic . . . puppy-dog-eyed, kinda sweet, knows-me-better-than-anyone-on-the-planet Evan. Uh-oh. When we finally do talk, will he be able to tell from my voice that I'm feeling all weird and confused about him? I decided I better not call him back just yet. If he really wants to speak to me, he'll call again, right?

UGH. Seriously, I feel like such a mess. Luckily, the one person who I can pretty much talk to about all this was just a phone call away.

"You still haven't spilled the beans about Katie being here, right?" I blurted out when Lanie picked up the phone.

"Well, hello to you, too!" said Lanie. "And no, I haven't. I've got bigger things to think about."

I figured it would take her about two seconds to launch into the latest Dustin story (and I realized it was best to let her get all her Dustin stuff out before I launched into my stuff—that way I'd get her full and undivided attention). But I didn't even have to wait **THAT** long.

GIVE ME A 171!

"It's over," Lanie moaned. I heard the telltale "oomph" sound that told me she had collapsed dramatically back onto her bed.

"What is over?" I asked, even though I was sure I knew the answer. I prayed to myself that Lanie had figured out that she and Dustin were not meant to be. I mean, how long was this Dustin Lovefest supposed to go on?

"I just read on a very credible blog that Dustin Barker has a girlfriend."

"I'm sorry, sweetie. But . . . you're surprised, why?" I asked.

"I'm not surprised. I'm depressed."

"Oh, well, in that case," I joked. "Look, I'll be home in a day, and we can do a whole Sad Romantic Comedy, Eat Lots of Junk Food, Mourn the Loss of Your Love Day. Deal?"

"Ok. It's just, you don't understand what it's like to be rejected. You already have a guy who likes you."

I couldn't help but smile at that. If she only knew. Yeah, Bevan likes me, but something changed for me, and I don't have a clue what. But she was so super sad I decided to wait until I was back to tell her what's going on with Bevan and me. The good thing was just hearing her voice made me feel a little better.

GIVE ME A 172!

"Lanie, give me a little credit. I can totally feel your pain. Even if it IS over, well, Dustin Barker."

"Mean," said Lanie. "The blog said that Dustin and this girl Crystal Myers, who opened for his concert, have been going out for a month! They even shared a soda the other day at In-N-Out Burger!"

"Just think of all the cute non-famous boys who are out there. I met a few really cute guys when I was out with Katie. They were super artsy and cool—and talked about books and music and stuff.

"I'm sure all Dustin talks about is himself. Just look at some of his interviews," I continued.

Lanie made a noise that sounded like humph. "Mads, people are supposed to talk about themselves when they're being interviewed."

"Good point," I said. "But still . . ."

"I know you're right," said Lanie. "Maybe I should move

to New York," she mused. "Then I can meet all those cute boys you're talking about."

I almost wanted to blurt out, "Cool, then you and I can both be artists and brood together in cafés all the time." But I remembered that I haven't even told her about the possibility of moving to New York yet either. Despite my original plan, it was clear Lanie definitely could **NOT** handle any of my news in her current emotional state. I'll just have to wait till I get home and really catch up with Lanie and tell her everything.

Sigh. I hate the waiting game ☹.

GIVE ME A 174!

SSSSSSSHHHHHhhhh...

Saturday, January 7

Afternoon, the no-tell hotel

Spirit Level:

Going Ho Ho Home!

Homeward bound! My suitcase is packed, and I said a little good-bye to my tiny hotel room. It almost feels like a second home by now—like if my room in Port Angeles had a baby, this is what it would look like. I even think I'm going to miss it.

I wrote a quick text to Katarina, wishing her good luck studying. This is the final home stretch—the test is just a few days away. And I really, really hope she passes.

Then I called Jacqui, hoping she'd answer, since I don't have much time before we leave for the airport. It took forever, but she finally picked up on, like, ring twelve.

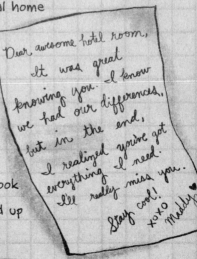

Dear awesome hotel room,
It was great knowing you. I know we had our differences, but in the end, I realized you've got everything I need. I'll really miss you.
Stay cool!
xoxo Maddy

GIVE ME A 175!

"So what's the feeling? You think Katarina will pass?" I asked her.

"Matt, Tabitha Sue, and I spent all last night studying with her. She said she feels ready, but I could tell she was nervous. We all are. The team has even started saying bad words in Russian."

I still feel a little guilty about not being there for all of this.

"Well, my fingers are crossed."

"You on your way home?" asked Jacqui.

"Yes, finally! It's been awesome, but I'm ready. I miss everyone."

"We miss you, too!" said Jacqui.

Awww . . .

I sat at the little hotel room desk and tried to think one last time before I left about what it would feel like to live here. I guess I won't really know until/if it happens. I tried to imagine Dad's new apartment, and me waking up in the morning to go to my new arts school. Of course, I'd be wearing the most amazing outfit because I'd be living in New York: the land of ah-mazing outfits.

GIVE ME A 176!

A knock on my door snapped me out of my daydream. "Who is it?" I asked.

"It's me, Katie."

I opened the door to see Katie with her backpack on and her suitcase behind her. "I was just leaving to get in a cab with Mom. But I wanted to say bye first."

"Cool." I smiled. "When's your flight?"

"At noon," she said.

"Oh, ours is at three. Too bad, we could have been on the plane together."

"That would have been fun," she said, smiling.

"So . . ."

"So . . ."

Talk about awkward. I was thinking that even though neither of us would admit it, this moment would probably be the last time we'd hang out as friends. It was a little bit of a bummer.

AWKWARD!

GIVE ME A
177!

"So, when do you find out about the auditions?" I asked, trying to fill the silence.

"Oh, it'll probably be at least a month or so before they decide."

"Wow," I said. "That'll build the anticipation, huh?"

Katie nodded. She fiddled with the straps on her backpack. "Whenever you want more of those cheer lessons, let me know."

"You really mean that?" I asked. I couldn't help it. The offer IS really tempting. . . .

"Yeah, I do," said Katie. "Oh, and I know I've said it a million times, but please, please don't tell anyone I was here."

"Your secret's safe," I said, making the "zipping the lips" motion with my fingers. The whole don't-tell-anyone thing is starting to make me feel über uncomfortable, though. First of all, I've already told two people. And now I'm lying to Katie about it, and promising to keep even more secrets from people when I get back home. But I guess what they say is true: What happens in New York stays in New York. (People totally say that, right?)

And then she did something completely out of character. She hugged me—the way she and Clementine and Hilary always hug when they see each other or

GIVE ME A 178!

leave each other. Like in that casual way friends say good-bye. I was so surprised I even jumped a little. Katie Parker-expressing warm and fuzzy feelings for moi. No one will believe it. (Not like I can TELL anyone, anyway.)

I decided to call Bevan before finally heading downstairs. It was time. I had to stop avoiding the weirdness, no matter what it would bring about.

"So . . . you hang out with those friends again?" he asked. He sounded a little jealous. Whoa!

"No, it was just that one time. But there were so many times I wished that you had been here this week. There were so many things you would have loved to see."

That's when I realized: OMG, that was a total lie!! It wasn't Bevan who I wanted to show the city to. It was Evan! How did THAT happen?

"Really?" I could hear the doubt and hope in his voice.

"Of course!" I said. The words just kept falling out of my mouth. Kind of the way food usually does, but this was actually WAY worse. I felt like I was going to turn into Pinocchio any minute.

Now I'm not just a liar, I'm a big FAT liar. Why can't my lame brain work any faster to determine these things BEFORE I start saying things I don't

GIVE ME A
179!

mean?? Maybe I should just stay in New York after all. That way I'll never have to tell Bevan that I'm not sure I feel the same way I used to, I'll never have to tell Evan that I'm having weird (and completely unacceptable!) feelings for him, **AND** I'll never have to choose between the Titans and the Grizzlies. Good plan!

"Have a good flight, Mads," said Bevan. "One that doesn't involve cat ladies or movies that make you cry," he added.

Awww, he remembered. Now I felt even worse.

AFTERNOON, UP IN THE AIR (TAKE TWO)

I was not looking forward to having time to think about things on the plane. Luckily, in the airport I found a rad (see, I can use it too!) book of really hard crosswords (except small note to self: In the future, try to use "rad" to describe something cooler than crossword puzzles) to keep me busy. This time I had a whole row of seats to myself. Bevan was right: No cat ladies = score!

And T.G., time flew by (ha-ha, get it?)! I mean, I was definitely thinking about stuff, especially the moving-to-New-York part, but sometimes all the thinking in the world can't help you. Sometimes you just need to feel it, you know? Sometimes no matter what

GIVE ME A
180!

your head says, you just have to go with your heart. As I watched the plane inch slowly toward Port Angeles on the little map screen on my personal TV monitor, my heart felt like it was swelling inside my chest, and the butterflies in my tummy began to buzz. Every little centimeter the plane moved made me feel a little more at ease.

I'm almost home ☺ .

And by the time the nose of the digital plane was almost on Fairchild International Airport, I knew my decision about New York versus Port Angeles was made. New York is completely awesome, but I'm not ready to leave what I have at home. At least not yet. Cheer, friends, Mom. I guess it took me leaving to really appreciate what I have.

Woohoo! Gotta put my tray table up and fasten my seat belt. I'm almost there!

GIVE ME A 18!!

Monday, January 9

Late afternoon, jeepers creepers, where'd you get those bleachers?

Holiday Spirit Level:

What Do You Love? Why Do You Love It? It's Home!

When I got home Saturday night, I was so tired I barely remember walking in and putting my bags down. But I **DO** know that Mom came into my room before I fell asleep, and we got to talk a little. I told her about Dad's move to New York. She was surprised, but not shocked.

"He deserves a lucky break," Mom said unexpectedly. I thought she'd be annoyed that he was going so far away from me. From us, I guess. "Your dad works so hard, I'm glad his company recognized how much he does for them." She smiled as she idly ran her hands over my comforter.

"There's something else." GULP. "He kind of asked me if I would want to come live with him and Beth. In New York," I said.

I saw Mom's whole body tense up as soon as the

GIVE ME A
182!

words escaped my lips. She didn't want me to notice, I could tell, but she was boiling with anger that he hadn't asked her about asking me first. I feel kind of bad now. I mean, Mom just said all these nice things about Dad, and then I went ahead and ruined it by telling her something to make her hate him again. On the other hand, perhaps that's just the universe righting itself again.

"Ok," she finally replied. "So, what do you think about that?"

She deserves definite props for trying to be all casual and cool about it.

"I'm thinking New York City is the most amazing place in the world."

I saw Mom's face fall.

"But," I rushed to finish my thought, "Port Angeles is my home, and I'd miss it too much to leave. And I'd miss <u>you</u> too much."

"Oh, Madington!" she gushed. "That's the sweetest thing you've ever said to me!"

"But I'm pretty sure I'd want to go to college there. Like, maybe FIT."

"Oh," said Mom, suddenly tensing up again. "College. Boy, that's way too far away to be thinking about yet! But whatever you decide," she finished, trying to be cheerful.

GIVE ME A 183!

"G'night, Mom," I said.

"Sleep tight," she said, as she closed my bedroom door.

After that I don't even remember hitting the pillow. New York wore me out!

I can't believe I'm saying this, but I couldn't wait to get to school today. I felt like I hadn't seen anyone in forever (well, cuz I hadn't). I mean, it had been so long, I almost forgot my locker combo! I was probably the only person in the whole class who actually skipped up the steps to the school today. It is the first day back from winter break, after all. All around me people look grumpy, because instead of sleeping late and watching movies all day they have to listen to their teachers talk and give them homework assignments.

Lanie met me by the Lounge, and I finally got to tell her everything—well, almost. I didn't tell her about the Evan thing, but I told her everything else: about Dad wanting me to move to New York. About how I wasn't sure I felt the same about Bevan anymore. She was really relieved I'm not thinking about moving, unless, and I quote, "You plan on packing me in your suitcase!"

"Hmmm, maybe it's just something in the air that's going around, you know?" she remarked, referring to

GIVE ME A
184!

the news of Bevan and my romance kind of souring out—at least in my mind.

"Um, are you saying what I think you're saying?" I asked. "Did the Dustin crush finally set sail??" I couldn't help the excitement that rang out in my voice.

"Actually, yup," Lanie said proudly. "All the blogs today are talking about how that girlfriend of his has been outed as a lip-syncher. I totally knew all along, ever since I heard her sing on one of his concert specials. But Dustin was shocked. You can see the pictures of how upset he is all over the Internet."

"Ok," I said. "I get it. Lip-synching is very uncool. But that doesn't explain why Dustin's been x-ed out of your love list."

"Boy, that New York air must have gotten to you, huh? Anyone who's shocked to discover that Crystal Myers lip-synchs is an idiot! The fact that he thought she was for real means he doesn't deserve my love."

"Whatever it took, I celebrate your newfound liberation!" I told her.

By the afternoon, I still hadn't seen Evan yet. We'd texted briefly yesterday, but today will be the first time I get to see him since before I left. (PS—He usually wanders by the Lounge on Monday mornings right around the time I was there with Lanie, but **THIS** morning he

GIVE ME A 185!

was nowhere to be found! Go figure!)

OF COURSE I ran into Bevan on my way to Mr. Hobart's. When I saw him talking to one of his soccer friends outside my math class, I hoped maybe he wouldn't catch me walking by. Well, first I hoped that seeing him would somehow shock my system and re-spark the flame that had died such a painful death in my heart. No such luck on either front.

"Hey, Mads!" he said, and waved. I waved back. He did one of those fist-slap-into-a-bro-hug things with his friend. "Later, bro," he said.

Then he walked up to me, his hands in his pockets, his shoulders hunched. He looked a little, ummm . . . nervous.

But by some strange twist of fate, I suddenly had this crazy delayed reaction. I was just standing there, looking into his eyes (dreading what I was going to say to him), when that feeling I had just over a week ago came flooding through me again. Those espresso-colored eyes are truly a force to be reckoned with. And just like that, I decided I didn't have to say anything at all. At least not just yet.

"So, how's it being back?" he asked.

I couldn't answer right away, because my eyes had drifted from his eyes to his hair, and I was too busy

GIVE ME A
186!

thinking about how cute it looked when it fell into his face like that. How does he do that? Magic?

"It's, um . . . good, actually," I said. "I'm glad to be home. Listen, I'm sorry I didn't call you."

He shrugged. "No big deal," he said. "I've been busy, anyway."

"Oh, yeah?"

"What?" He smiled. "Don't look so surprised."

I looked down at my shoes. "I'm not surprised. Sorry."

Well, I **WAS** surprised, but not about him being able to entertain himself while I was away. I was surprised that I still seem to have some feelings for Bevan. I thought I'd left them all on that plane to New York.

"You want to hang out tomorrow?"

"Sure," I said. "We can meet up after practice, as usual?" At least one more hang-out session is in order, to determine the full extent of my feelings. Right?

"Yeah, sounds great." He looked at his watch. "Ack,

GIVE ME A 187!

I'm late. Later, skater," he said coolly, before jogging away to class.

I leaned against my locker, letting this all sink in. Great, yet another thing to be confused about. And I still couldn't find E anywhere. Was he avoiding me?

By the end of the day, there was still no sign of him. So I headed to the gym to meet Jacqui before practice so she could catch me up on what I missed last week. As soon as I walked through those heavy doors, that familiar smell of stinky shoes and sweat filled me with happiness. My gym! They should bottle this stuff.

I could see that Katie, Clementine, and Hilary had the same idea as us. They were stretching in their corner of the gym and laughing at something Clementine said. I tried to make eye contact with Katie, but she seemed too busy to look in our direction. Or maybe she didn't want to. Who knows? It's what I expected. Sad, but true.

Jacqui told me about some of the drills she made

GIVE ME A 188!

the squad do during the week. "And everyone knows the new routine by now!" she said with pride. "Even Matt and Ian finally got into it."

"Awesome!" I said. I couldn't wait to see it at practice. And I really couldn't wait to see my teammates.

Jacqui and I practiced some more advanced stuff, and I showed her some of the moves Katie had taught me that week.

"Where did you learn that?" asked Jacqui, when I showed her the new technique Katie had taught me to make my scorpion even better.

I was about to say, "Katie showed me," when I caught myself. This was my promise to Katie. That I won't tell anyone about New York.

"Oh. Got bored. Watched a lot of YouTube cheer videos in my hotel room," I lied.

"Cool."

So I guess I am going to keep this Katie secret from Jacqui and the team. It's probably better not to stir up any more drama for myself anyway. I have quite the full plate already.

As I was stretching on the mat, someone practically pummeled me from behind. "Tabitha Sue!" I exclaimed, when I realized who it was.

GIVE ME A 189!

she gave me a giant bear hug. "I missed you, Mads!"

"I missed you, too!" I said.

Jared came running up to me. "I heard you saw Spider-Man," he said. "Did you just die? How great is the choreography?" He brought his hand to his forehead like he was fainting. "Best musical of the year," he said.

"It was great," I agreed. "The music was great."

The team showed me what they did last week— and how much they improved the new routine. They rocked! Diane is just as great as Jacqui said—she was practically leading everyone else through the more advanced moves. Jared was smiling at her the whole time like a proud parent. Katarina did cast a lot of nervous glances at Diane, though. I know she is dying to know if she passed and if she'll be getting replaced or not. We all were. I wanted to talk to Jacqui about just telling the team that Diane could compete with us either way, but the timing wasn't quite right. I just got back, so I figured I should wait at least one practice before making any major announcements.

But practicing and leading the team today with Jacqui felt so good—like when we'd first started training together. I almost forgot what it was like to train with her. How we can challenge each other to our limits, and hours can go by without us realizing it

GIVE ME A
190!

because we're having so much fun. While I was in New York, it was so easy to see myself going to school there and hanging with all the city kids talking art 24/7. But now that I'm back, it feels like, "What was I thinking? Cheer is so your thing." Maybe there are small things I can do to work fashion design back into my life. Like subscribing to a super-fashion-focused mag or signing up for a fun design course at the Cultural Center. And I need to keep expanding my knowledge by trying new patterns and making stuff other than cheer uniforms. But at least being home has shown me that I'm not ready to leave cheer completely. **EVEN** for a super-snazzy arts school and a super-cool New York Life. Not yet, at least.

NIGHT, MY ROOM

Ok, so I finally saw Evan. Yeah, I literally ran smack into him on my way out of the gym after practice. He was just about to open the doors himself. It was, like, an "OUCH, is your head ok?" kind of smack. I have a habit of doing that, I guess—running into people. Anyway, he was in the library doing some research for another edition of SuperBoy, but decided to leave and come find me after practice.

"I was wondering when I'd see you," I said, feeling a

GIVE ME A 1911!

little flustered (and bruised ☹).

He was wearing a cute flannel shirt and too-small-for-his-frame jeans. He was smiling from ear to ear. In other words, he looked **ADORBS** in his odd little way.

"Really? I was looking for you all day."

When he said that, I felt my face get red and hot. It was so weird to go from wondering if he even wanted to be my friend anymore to having him say something like that.

"No, you weren't."

"Uh. Yes I was. Ask Lanie."

I hadn't seen Lanie since the morning. So I had to believe him.

"Ok, you win," I said, smiling.

"So how was New York?" he asked.

I sighed heavily. "It was fun, but it was exhausting. I'm happy to be home."

"Me too," Evan said. Then he shook his head. "I mean, I'm glad you're back."

We stood there awkwardly for a few moments, and then I remembered the book I bought him. I kneeled down to get it out of my bag. When I looked back at him, he was looking at me funny.

"Here," I said, to break the silence.

Evan opened the book to the title page, where the

GIVE ME A
192!

author had written his autograph. The next thing I knew, Evan's arms were around me. "Thanks, Mads," he said softly into my neck, then quickly pulled away.

"Sorry," he said, blushing. "I just . . . uh . . . I really wanted that book."

Just then Jacqui burst through the gym doors. "Hey, Evan," she said, completely oblivious to what was going on between us. Not that THAT much was going on. Just, you know, that she interrupted a hug, or whatever.

"Mads, you want a ride home?" she asked, stretching her triceps over her head. She looked from me to Evan. "We can drop you off too, Evan."

Evan backed away. "No, I'm ok. My mom's on her way," he said. "But thanks. Talk to you later, Mads?" he asked.

I nodded. I hadn't said a word since the hug.

"Cool," he said, walking backward a few steps with his hands in his pockets, before sprinting down the hall.

I realized I'd been holding my breath since the moment he'd hugged me.

"You ok there?" asked Jacqui.

"Yeah," I said, picking my backpack up off the floor. "Just tired from practice. It's been a while, you know?"

Jacqui looked at me funny but didn't ask any

GIVE ME A
193!

questions. I was totally relieved.

When I got home, Mom was sitting at the kitchen table with the cordless phone. "Ok, thanks so much," I heard her say as I put my coat away. "That's great news."

I took a seat next to her, where there was a place setting for one. She'd already eaten but had made me one of her favorite "easy dinners": a TLT (turkey bacon, lettuce, tomato). I took a big bite and realized how hungry I was.

When she hung up the phone, I was like, "So? What's great news?"

She didn't hesitate before telling me that Katarina had passed the test. Woohoo!! That makes one less complicated thing in my life. The Grizzlies will be back in the Get Up and Cheer Competition, and Katarina is safe. Hooray!

We gave each other a high five.

"That's awesome!" I said. "Ooh, I'm going to call her." I picked up my phone.

"You'll have to wait till tomorrow," said Mom, grabbing the phone from me playfully. "We're not supposed to know. I literally begged her teacher to tell me."

"Mom! That's pretty nosy of you," I said.

"I know, I know. But I couldn't wait. And guess

GIVE ME A 194!

what? She got an A-!" Mom said, shaking her fists like she was waving two pom-poms. "You have to keep it a secret. I promised I wouldn't tell Katarina."

"Secret's safe," I promised. If there's a skill I've gotten a lot of practice with lately, it's secret keeping.

"Guess if Diane wants to stay, we'll just have an extra person on the team," I said.

Mom nodded. "She's a nice addition, though, don't you think?"

"Yeah. She's great at stunts. I mean, it will be weird to have someone else on the team, but I guess things always work out the way they're supposed to," I said, taking the last bite of my sandwich.

"Hmm, that's quite a mature attitude," Mom said. "It's very Zen."

"One of the many things I learned on vacation," I replied.

After I did the dishes, I went up to my room to call Lanes, but she wasn't around. I saw that Evan was on chat, and so was Bevan. Both of them wrote to me at the exact same second! They must have been waiting for me to get online, I guess. I sat and stared at both message boxes, trying to decide who to talk to first.

But you know what? I am **SO SICK** of making decisions right now. So instead, I just signed off chat

GIVE ME A
195!

altogether. I collapsed onto my bed and grabbed my lucky pom-pom, curling the strands around my fingers as I stared up at the ceiling. I thought about that hug earlier today. When Evan wrapped his arms around me, I got all tingly. I did! There's no denying it. I felt like little particles of electricity were jumping all over my skin. It was definitely more intense than what I felt when I saw Bevan earlier today. No matter how cute he is.

I mean, I obviously like Bevan. But . . . the way I feel about Evan is something . . . deeper. Like he knows me inside and out. Well, of course I feel that way—he's my **BEST FRIEND**. Or . . .

GIVE ME A 196!

This can't really be happening. Am I going crazy? Or has my BFF Evan become **NOT** just my BFF anymore? Can he really be . . . a certified **CRUSH**?

Rah, rah, aaaaaahhhhhhhh!

Whoa. I'm sooooooooooooo in trouble.

And something tells me SuperBoy can't fix this one.

Or can he???

GIVE ME A 197!

And now, an excerpt from
the next book in the series,
Bevan vs. Evan
(And Other School Rivalries)

Spirit Song Level:

Sweet Dreams Are Made of Cheer (usually)

OMG, I just had an MEM (mega embarrassing moment). There I was, innocently sitting at my desk in Mr. Cooper's class. I had my notes open on my desk (because I'm studious! Ha-ha) and my eyes were totally focused on what Mr. Cooper was writing on the board. I mean, I even noticed when he tried to pick a booger out of his nose but pretended he was just scratching an itch.

Well, the thing is, I was **TRYING** to be totally focused on Mr. Cooper. But there was a tiny problemo: I was totally exhausted! My eyes kept doing that droopy thing and my body would start to sway, and then I'd pinch myself to get alert again.

"Can someone describe some of the ways in which Boo Radley's character represents the theme of innocence in <u>To Kill a Mockingbird</u>?"

asked Mr. Cooper. He looked around the classroom expectantly. Luckily, he didn't look at me.

Jeremiah Ramirez waved his hand in the air frantically. Typical. He looked like he was straining to give his answer. Like if he wasn't picked, he might actually pass out.

"Has anyone besides Jeremiah done their homework?" Mr. Cooper asked wearily. He let out a big sigh. "Ok, Jeremiah, yes?"

And just as Jeremiah was giving his answer, I must have passed out because suddenly I wasn't in class anymore. I wasn't even **ME** anymore. I was Boo Radley (Yikes! A dude!), sitting in a courtroom dressed in a Titans uniform.

Tabitha Sue Stevens (one of my Grizzly teammates) was the prosecutor, and she was pointing at me and yelling something. Then I realized that the whole jury was made up of the Grizzlies, who were shouting at me.

"Traitor!" the crowd yelled. "How dare you switch teams!"

"But you don't understand!" I said (not as myself but as Boo Radley, of course). "I can explain!"

And here is the mega embarrassing part: I must have been talking in my sleep because when I opened my eyes, Mr. Cooper was standing right over me, hairy nostrils flaring, and saying, "Madison Hays, would you like to explain specifically what the rest of us 'don't understand'?"

Oh no. I said that OUT LOUD?

I wiped the drool from the side of my mouth and heard some snickers echo around me. The ENTIRE CLASS was staring at me!!!

"Um, sorry, Mr. Cooper," I said, hoping the redness in my face wasn't too obvious.

He gave me an angry "hmph" and walked back to the front of the classroom. T.G.

Then Sylvie Harris was like, "Nice dream, Sleeping Beauty?"

Ugh. Wanted 2 die.

I should have known better than to have stayed up practically all night last night. No, I wasn't watching She's the Man for the millionth time or catching up on my Teen Vogues. Instead I was glued to YouTube, watching a gazillion cheer videos. Titan spring tryouts will be here before I know it. In a month, to be exact, and I need to be on point this time—I mean, if I do decide to audition.

It's not like I'm 100% ready to go to the Dark Side. I'm still torn about trying out at all, and what I would do if I even made the team. But ever since my New

York trip, when Katie Parker (capitán of los Titans!) planted the idea in my head that I'm some kind of super awesome cheerleader—Titan material even—I've been thinking about trying out for the Titans. Like, a lot.

Here's the major unfortunate thing: Katie had been all, "I'll train you when we get back home!" when we were in New York, but now that we're back, she's been treating me like I have the bubonic plague. (See? I pay attention in class.)

Just the other day I passed her sitting with Clementine Prescott (Titan Triumvirate #2) and Hilary Cho (Titan Triumvirate #3) on the way to my table in the caf, and even though she hasn't been so nice since we got back from New York, I couldn't help but give her a smile as I walked by. The entire table was SILENT as I made my way past them. The kind of silent that makes you feel like maybe they've been talking about you (and PS—it wasn't about how great your outfit looked that day). And as soon as I passed them, they all burst out laughing. Luckily, I didn't have to slink away like a giant loser to sit by myself. My BFFs Lanie and Evan were already at our table, so I hightailed it to them, trying to hide my beet-red face behind my lunch tray.

So anyway, Katie's 'tude means that my tryout for the Titans is all on me. Well, obviously whether I make the team or not is my problem, but it would have been nice if Katie decided to live up to her promise of training me. In the meantime I've been secretly studying up on the Titans: rereading their Spirit Rules book, watching videos of Titan practices and competitions, and dropping by some of their practices. Last night I watched their Regionals routine for about the thousandth time. If I'm going to have a chance of kicking butt at tryouts, I know I'll have to be able to do everything on that video. That is, if I do end up trying out. I haven't even told anyone I'm thinking about it yet. And I **CANNOT** tell the Grizzlies, like, ever. I feel terrible keeping this big secret from my team. This secret makes me feel, like, the opposite of being a team player. It is sooooo hard going to Grizzly practices knowing that my mind is slightly focused on another team. Talk about **NOT** being a team player, how about being a traitor co-captain! Wonder what Mr. Cooper would have had to say about my problem had I actually answered his question earlier today?

LATER THAT DAY, SNARKING IN THE PARKING LOT

Um. Yeah. So let's just say I wasn't at my best today during practice. I feel like dog poop. By my last class of the day I could feel myself slipping into dreamland again, so I spent most of class pinching my arm and stabbing my hand with the tip of my pencil (works like a charm, BTW). I couldn't imagine how I'd make it through practice. I went over to the vending machine and bought one of those crazy energy drinks that claim to turn you into Road Runner (meep meep!) for five hours. "Yeah," I said to myself. "That's exactly what I need to get through practice."

It worked for, like, five minutes. For five whole minutes (basically, the time it took me to get ready for Grizzly practice), I felt a blast of energy course through my veins. I tore open my locker while untying my hot pink Cons, and at the same time started doing a leg stretch.

"Hey, Maddy, you ok?" asked Tabitha Sue. She was looking at me funny (I'm sensing a pattern here . . . more on that later).

"Yeah!" I exclaimed. I practically ripped off the cute Empire waist top I was wearing and started to put on my shorts. "Never been better!"

Tabitha Sue pointed at my legs. "You sure?"

I looked down. Oops. Forgot to take my pants off. That would help, huh?

I blushed, embarrassed. "Thanks, Tabitha Sue. I just

had an energy drink, and I feel like I can't do anything fast enough."

Tabitha Sue tightened a shoelace and shook her head. "Well, enjoy it while it lasts. Those things can make you crash. Hard."

Tabitha Sue was sooooooo right. By the time I moseyed into the gym, I could feel my energy draining out of me like a leaky faucet. I was dragging my feet by the time I reached the rest of the team.

I did my best to be perky for warm-up, but by the time we got to practicing round-offs with the team, I was yawning like it was my job. I know this isn't, like, the biggest deal in the world. People have tired days all the time. It's just that I **ALWAYS** have energy for cheer. So when I have an off day, it's really obvious.

Jacqui and I divided the teams into groups of two to practice round-offs. We've been working on them forever, but still, some peeps have been a little sloppy on the finish. I was in charge of Jared and Ian. Jared began his running start and then went into a hurdle before turning upside down. I totally should have seen it coming—his arms weren't high enough in the hurdle, and he was going too slowly into the round-off. I also should have been spotting him, but since my brain was mush, I was standing off to the side. Bad captain!

Jared bounced on his butt and landed with his legs splayed out on the floor.

"Ow!" he squeaked. "Someone help me up."

I rushed over to his side and told him not to move. Jacqui came running over too.

"You ok?" she asked, her forehead crinkling with worry.

Jared sighed dramatically. "I think I bruised my ego."

Jacqui laughed. "All right, easy getting up. Go get some water."

I patted Jared on the back. "Sorry, dude. That was totally my fault. I should have been spotting you."

"No worries," he said, as he limped away.

I knew Jacqui would have something to say about this. I was right.

"Mads, what happened?" she asked. "You don't seem yourself today."

I shook my head. "No, I'm not. I'm really sorry. I was up tossing and turning all night. I slept for, like, two hours."

"Something wrong?" she asked, searching my face for an answer.

I laughed. "Nah." I shrugged. "Not really. Just, you know, Bevan stuff." It wasn't a total lie. I had been thinking about me and Bevan a lot lately, but more on that later.

Jacqui smiled. "Oh, totally. I hope everything's ok with you guys."

When it comes to guy stuff, you don't have to say much. Your girls just automatically understand.

I nodded my head, hoping she'd change the subject.

"But listen, Mads, you have to keep it together during practice. Jared could have gotten hurt."

"Yeah, I know. I'm really sorry."

I forced myself to bring my A-game to the rest of practice. But I think after what happened with Jared, the rest of the team wasn't super eager to do anything aerial without Jacqui around. I don't exactly blame them.

Diane somewhat saved the day when she asked if she could show us a new move she learned from a cheerleader friend back in her old town. I'm happy that she decided to stay on the team even after Katarina passed her social studies test and we didn't end up needing a backup member after all. It's cool having another person with a solid gymnastics background on the squad.

"All right, guys, you've probably heard of the punch front," said Diane. "But since we haven't done it yet, I thought I'd show you."

Side note: A punch front is basically a front flip,

using both feet to take off from. I'm pretty sure we started to learn this before Diane got here, but no one was near mastering it.

"Ok, so first I'm gonna show you how it looks, and then I'll break it down."

We all cleared some space to give Diane room. Diane took a breath and, without any momentum, flipped in the air, landing perfectly. Not a wobble in sight. Nice!

Jared started clapping, and the rest of the team followed suit.

"Thanks, Diane!" said Jacqui. "Maybe we can all work on this one, huh, guys?"

Everyone looked game, though Jared and Tabitha Sue both had slightly freaked-out looks on their faces. I love it when the team is pumped about learning new things. We divided up again into groups to practice the move. Out of the corner of my eye I saw Katie and Hilary walking into the gym. I learned my lesson from before, not to smile or wave or anything (unless I have a big desire to feel like a loser). So I pretended not to notice her. But then she turned her head and saw me and she actually **ROLLED HER EYES** at me! Can you believe?? What did I do to her? I'm racking my brain to figure it out. I know we smoothed things over a superloooooong time ago about the Bevan thing, and that also laid the Evan thing to rest too. (Wow, do I sense a pattern here?) So that isn't it. What can it be? List time!

* Did I toilet paper her house? No.
* Did I come to school dressed in the same outfit as her? Hardly.
* Did I spill orange juice on her pants at lunchtime so that it might look like she had a different kind of accident? Negative.

Speaking of Bevan, I don't really want to admit it to myself, but I don't have a choice anymore: This thing with Bevan is bothering me way more than I thought it would. Maybe it's the exhaustion speaking, but I'm a teeny-weeny bit upset that he's been so MIA since I got back. I don't really get it—before I went away, we were like **THIS CLOSE!**

But since I got back we have barely made any plans, and I basically see Mr. Hobart more than I see him. (Which is totally unfortunate, because Bevan is way cuter than Mr. Hobart.)

I couldn't help but look for him in the hall when I left the gym. He used to practically always meet me after practice, which I loved because it was never a planned thing. He'd just be there. Lately, I guess he's been mucho busy with soccer stuff. I don't think that team even leaves the gym. Maybe they set up sleeping bags and work out until they all fall asleep on the gym floor?

I totally get being obsessed with a sport (I mean, hello!) but still, it's annoying that his obsession is affecting **ME**! I don't like being the thing that gets thrown to the curb. I think what really sucks is that I'm kind of not sure if I feel the same way I did about him before, and the less I see him, the more true that realization becomes. It's totally not his fault that I had a **BIG EUREKA** moment about my feelings for Evan while I was away. But it would help if we actually spent some time together—because then I could actually figure out if I feel more for Evan than I do for Bevan or vice versa.

All right, my brain is now officially closed for the night. I can't take anymore today! Can't wait to get home and just **CRASH!**

NIGHT, CHILLAXING IN MY ROOM

Are you there, cheer gods? It's me, Madison! Oh wait. You're actually LISTENING?! Guess so, because right after I inhaled a delish meatball sub and lay down comatose on my bed, I saw I had a **MISSED CALL!**

Lo and behold, it was from Bevan. He left me a voicemail and everything! I was half expecting an automated message, like (cue robot voice that mispronounces everything), "Hello. Madisone. This is an automatic message from Bev and Ramsey. I am sorry that I have not called you in many days. Soccer has taken. Over my life." But luckily, it wasn't automatic. It was **THE BEVAN RAMSEY** in the flesh (or in the voice, I should say) asking me to call him when I got a chance.

I called him back, and he picked up. I'm so awkward at leaving messages, so I was really glad.

"Whadup, Madison?" he said. "You got my message?"

"Yeah, I did. What's goin' on?" I asked, trying to be über-casual. Which was the opposite of what I was feeling inside. In my head I was like, "Where have you been for the past few weeks? Why have I become yesterday's news?"

"Listen, I'm uh . . . sorry I've been such a stranger lately," he said awkwardly.

"What do you mean?" I asked, totally lying. Duh! Like I haven't noticed.

"Well, you know. We haven't been hanging out much lately. My team is really bringing things to the next level. Wait, so, you haven't, like, noticed?"

I might be wrong, or imagining things (wouldn't be a first!), but I think he actually sounded a little hurt. Like he wanted me to notice and care that we hadn't chilled in a while. I don't know why I didn't just tell him that I was kinda upset that he's been so busy. Maybe I didn't feel like letting him see that he hurt my feelings.

"Yeah," I said. "I guess. You're right, it's been a while. It sounds like you've been really busy."

Awkward pause.

"So. Yeah," he continued. "I was wondering if you wanted to, um, go bowling Friday night?"

Bowling? How cute! Bevan had told me he's only been bowling, like, once in his life. So I guess he's not afraid to look stupid in front of me. I'd told him I'd show him a thing or two.

"Yeah, I think I'm free," I said (playing hard to get, ha-ha). "Let's do it."

"Cool."

"Cool."

"So, I'll see you at school tomorrow?" he asked.

"Yep. I don't plan on being a delinquent."

I was glad he called, but then, for some reason, I decided to go online and see who was there. And now I realize, I wasn't just looking to see if "just anyone" was there. My mind had wandered to Evan. Before I had a chance to IM him, a message popped up on my screen.

Here's our convo:

Evan: "Hey u!"

My heart actually skipped a beat. What is happening to me?

Maddy: "Hi!"

Evan: "Whatchu up 2?"

Maddy: "Meh. Not much. Just hangin'. Soooo tired."

Evan: "Grueling Grizzly practice?"

Ugh. I hate lying, but I'm not ready to tell him about my plan to possibly try out for the Titans.

Maddy: "Yuppers."

Evan: "☺."

Maddy: "Totes."

Evan: "U should relax. I'll check on u l8r."

He is sooo sweet, thinking about me like that.

We said good-bye and signed off. Finally! Time to really pass out. I closed my computer and went to take off my earrings. When I looked in the mirror, I saw that I was smiling ear to ear.

And you know what? This smile isn't from Bevan asking me out to go bowling. It's from talking to Evan!!! Gah! Cray-zee-ness.

Song Level:

Titans on My Mind

This morning I was still in a pretty good mood from my convo with Evan last night, PLUS the fact that Bevan actually acknowledged that I exist and asked me out for tomorrow. Things were going well for little ol' moi, Madison Hays. I ate a delish breakfast (Pop-Tarts all the way), tried to ignore the goofy way Mom was been acting all morning (parents are weird), AND when we got in the car, my fave song was on the radio (I heart Bruno Mars). Not a bad start to the day, right?

Sigh. Little did I know that surprises awaited me at the school of Doom. I sashayed through the big clonking doors at school and found myself face-to-face with a poster. It wasn't just an ordinary poster—nothing like those neon-colored flyers that people throw all over the school's walls advertising "Math Club Party!" or "Save the Lizards of Laos!" Nope. I was face-to-face with a poster for the annual Sunshine Dance that's just three weeks away.

Here's the thing: The Sunshine Dance is a **HUGE STINKING DEAL.** This isn't a girls-on-one-side-of-the-dance-floor-boys-on-the-other kind of dance. It's the first serious dance anyone ever goes to at our school. This will be my first time going to it. Everyone knows that people will be dressed in their absolute best outfits, and **EVERYONE** who plans on going will be going with a date.

As I stood there pondering my dilemma, two girls came skittering to a screeching halt in front of the poster.

"OMG!" one girl squealed. "Only a couple more weeks! And I don't even have shoes yet!"

Um. Shoes? I didn't even remember it was **HAPPENING** until two seconds ago.

"Seriously," her friend said. "You better get shopping before they're all out of cute stuff. I bought my dress and shoes months ago. And my dad reserved us a limo. Eeeeeee!"

Dress? Shoes? **LIMO?** I am so behind.

I walked in a daze toward my locker, wondering how I missed this. I'm sure people have been talking about this dance for weeks now, and I've just been oblivious. Really, how does something like this take me by surprise? Oh. Yeah. Right. Maybe it has something to do with my secret training for Titan tryouts. Guess I've been a little preoccupied (u think?) If there's one thing I like more than anything (or at least as much as cheer), it is dreaming up an outfit for a fun occasion. And this is the occasion of occasions!

I started to mentally flip through the pages of dresses that I've been dying to design but haven't had a reason to wear. (I've got quite a catalog up there.)

Suddenly, a voice interrupted me. "So did you see the posters are finally up?"

I turned to see Lanie, fighting hard to not be at all excited about the dance of the year. Dances and ordinary social events are not Lanie's thing. African dance? Yes. School dance? Not so much. HOWEVER, I know that deep down, Lanie Marks is just as excited as, say, Clementine Prescott is at the idea of getting glammed up (in Lanie's own way, of course) and maybe dancing with a boy. She is human, after all (or at least I think so).

"Yeah," I said, fiddling with my locker combination to jumble up the code. "Did you know this was coming so soon? Because those posters are the first I've heard of it."

Lanie rolled her eyes. "Have you been living under a

pom-pom? It's all anyone ever talks about these days. The excitement must be infectious or something, because brace yourself—I think I want to go."

"I can just see it now, you entering the dance in a sparkly hot-pink dress and breaking it down to a techno beat."

Lanie laughed. "Right. That's exactly what'll happen. So . . ." she looked at me expectantly. "I assume you'll be going with B?"

Funny . . . with all my excitement about the dress-up part of the dance, I hadn't even thought about the whole date part.

"Well, actually . . . not as of yet," I said, shaking my head with a frown. It seems I'm not the only one who's on Sunshine Dance delay. Hmph.

Lanie made a face like it was no biggie. "Well, you know Bevan. He's probably just been so into his sports that the dance hasn't made it to his brain yet."

I chewed the inside of my lip, trying to think back to our conversation last night. Why hadn't he just asked me then? Maybe he wanted to wait for our bowling date to ask me in person. . . .

"The good news is, he _finally_ asked me to go out on another date. I was starting to think he'd forgotten my screen name."

"Ooh, that's good," said Lanie, perking up. "Definitely a step in the dance direction," she added.

She must have seen me looking all distant because she quickly said, "Remember, he's a dude. Dudes don't live for things like dances. Not like girls do." She lowered her eyes. "I mean, girls except for me."

"Ok, Miss I-Think-I-Want-to-Go," I snarked.

Just then we saw everyone scurrying to class. "Guess we should mosey on to Torture Session Number One," I said.

Lanie patted me on the back. "He'll ask you, don't worry."

"Yeah, yeah . . . we'll see."

I was almost the last person to arrive at Mr. Hobart's class, and everyone knows that Mr. H is a total dragon about people being late. I once heard about this one kid who was always late. Mr. H made him solve every problem in a math book before he was allowed to leave detention. He actually made the kid come back the next afternoon to finish up! I'm actually surprised Mr. H didn't just make him spend the night. Imagine, having to spend a night with Mr. Hobart. Talk about a nightmare sleepover!

I took my usual seat three rows from the front of the classroom. It's been my seat this whole year.

The rule is, once you choose your seat on the first day, it becomes your designated spot (unofficially), so you better like it. I don't make up the rules; it's just the way it is here in Port Angeles. Katie and Clem, who are also in my class (lucky me!) have always sat diagonal from me. But lately, they've both moved to the extra chairs in the last row of the classroom. (Apparently, rules don't apply to them.) I have a feeling it has something to do with me because whenever Clem and Katie walk by, they snicker as they pass me, and practically sprint to their new seats. It's like I'm the kid who peed in her pants who everyone else wants to avoid.

Right after I sat down, Katie and Clem walked into class. Of course, **THEY** didn't seem to be in any kind of rush. Mr. Hobart has a soft spot for the Titans, so they sauntered in, taking their time. Clementine actually stopped by the window to gaze at her reflection and fluff her hair. Ugh.

So then, they both purposely walked past MY desk, which is totally unnecessary. As Clementine passed me, she mumbled "Ew," and Katie laughed.

I can't stand it anymore. **WHY, OH WHY, AM I THEIR NEW FAVORITE PUNCHING BAG?**

You're invited to a

CREEPOVER™

WE DARE YOU...
TO CHECK OUT THESE TERRIFIC AND TERRIFYING TALES!

CUPCAKE DIARIES

Middle school can be hard...
some days you need a cupcake.

Meet Katie, Mia, Emma, and Alexis—together they're the Cupcake Club. Check out their stories wherever books are sold or at your local library!

CUPCAKE DIARIES
Katie and the cupcake cure
by coco simon

CUPCAKE DIARIES
Mia in the mix
by coco simon

Did you **LOVE** this book?

Want to get access to great books for **FREE?**

Join

Simon & Schuster

IN THE

bookloop

<u>where you can</u>

✦ Read great books for FREE! ✦

❀ Get exclusive excerpts ❀

⸔ Chat with your friends ⸕

◉ Vote on polls ◉

Log on to ❀ everloop.com

and join the book loop group!